*I opened **The Last Perfect Summer**, as a favor to a friend, and couldn't put it down until I was through. It transported me to a time and place I had forgotten, and I had to wonder just who I would be today without my own memories of childhood. I missed a night of sleep, but didn't care. It's that good. A must read for the baby boomer generation*

~**Mark Razz**
92.5 XTU Radio, Philadelphia

I started crying in Chapter 32, when the old coach got up to give his pep talk before the championship game, and never stopped until two hours after I finished the book. And I haven't cried in twenty years.

~**Larry Kelly**
Radio Talk Show Host and
Pennsylvania "SUPER LAWYER"
New Castle, Pennsylvania

THE LAST PERFECT SUMMER

Windy City Publishers
2118 Plum Grove Rd., #349
Rolling Meadows, IL 60008
www.windycitypublishers.com

Published in the United States of America

First Edition: 2013

ISBN: 978-1-935766-42-1

Library of Congress Control Number: 2012951068

Cover Design by Adam Carter

This novel is dedicated to my wife,
Elizabeth Boschini Prence,
and to the town of Koppel, Pennsylvania.

THE LAST PERFECT SUMMER

BY ED PRENCE

The child is father of the man.
William Wordsworth, 1802

chapter one

Just Let Him Live

I stepped off the elevator and walked straight toward the nurses' station. So this was it, Mayview Hospital. I had no idea the place was so huge. I must have driven a mile across the complex to get to the building housing patients with chronic mental illness. I was surprised that it was so easy to get through the security gate. All the guard asked for was my name and who I wanted to visit. Then he just let me roll right through. I drove past ten or twelve buildings, including one completely surrounded by a high chain-link fence topped with razor-sharp barbed wire. *That must be the ward for the criminally insane*, I thought, *the ward that made Mayview famous.* "Poor Harry," I said out loud to no one, "How did it ever come to this?" Of course, Harry wasn't a criminal. He wasn't even insane. His "chronic mental illness" was caused by a bout with viral encephalitis fifteen years earlier. I remembered that he had run a temperature of 105 degrees for four days. "A virus in the brain," his doctors said. They were so sure he was going to die that they had let all his friends go into his room to say goodbye. But he didn't die. He lived. He was left with the intellect of a five-year-old, but he lived.

He was twenty-nine years old when he had "the attack," as his mother and wife called it. I can still remember them in the waiting room crying and praying. "Just let him live, God. Please, just let him live."

The lady behind the glass in the nurses' station was wearing a pink pastel flowered top and light green pants. I think she was a nurse, but I wasn't sure. *Why don't they just wear white?* I thought. *White shoes, white hose, white dress, and a little white hat. What was wrong with that?*

"I'm here to visit Harry Kirkland," I told her. "My name's Ted Tresh. I'm an old friend of his."

"Great!" she said with a big smile. "I'm sure he'll be happy to see you. But the patients are at lunch right now. Can you wait about half an hour?" I looked up at the clock behind her. It was 11:30. I hadn't visited Harry for over fifteen years and his mother had assured me he wouldn't even recognize me. "Sure, I can wait," I sighed. "Where should I go?"

"You can wait in his room," she said, still smiling broadly. "He's in 310. But you can't take that picture frame with you, sir. There's no glass allowed on this ward."

I had almost forgotten I was carrying the frame with the old news clipping in it. "It's a plastic frame," I told her, "plastic frame, clear plastic slide. There's no glass or metal in it." I handed it over to her for inspection. "I guess that'll be all right," she said brightly. Her smile was beginning to look pasted on her face. *I'll bet Harry hates this chick*, I thought. *He could always spot a phony.*

As I walked down the hallway, I thought of all the things on my agenda for the day. I was in advertising sales and had hours of proposals to write, contracts to close, and prospects to call. It was October, the peak of the Pittsburgh advertising cycle, and I had only allotted about sixty minutes for this visit to Harry. I was already behind schedule. *It's just going to have to wait*, I resolved. *If I can't take a couple hours a decade to visit an old friend, maybe I'm working too hard.*

I stepped into room 310 and hated it immediately. Although it was 1997, the walls were painted that putrid pale green color so popular with hospitals in the 1950s and 1960s. There were twin beds in the room. *He must have a roommate.* The thought made me a little uneasy. I was ready to deal with Harry's condition, but I wasn't sure about having a psychotic looking over his shoulder.

I walked around for a few minutes to size up the place. There were so many coats of green paint on the wall that the electrical outlets were nearly sealed shut. There were bars on the windows and a small private bathroom with a little pop-out push button on the outside of the door handle. "He can't even lock the door when he takes a piss," I said under my breath.

Finally I settled into the soft fake-leather chair in the corner and looked down at the old framed news clipping in my lap. All those smiling faces looking up at me, our Little League all-star team from 1964. Could it really have been as magical as I remember it? That summer, that perfect summer.

chapter two

The Pick-Up Game

"Hey, Teddeee." Every morning that summer started the same. "Hey, Teddeee." It was Sammy Bellissimo and Harry Kirkland outside my window at about nine o'clock.

My mother was one of the sweetest women on Earth. But for some reason all the kids were afraid to knock at our door. Instead they stood outside my bedroom window and kind of chanted my name over and over until I came outside.

My mother tapped at my bedroom door and stuck her head in the room. "Teddy, Nelson, your friends are waiting for you." Nelson was my brother, about a year and a half younger than me. We shared a bedroom. We also had two sisters, who shared another bedroom. It was 1964, the height of the baby boom. Our fathers had all fought in the Second World War then came home and found decent-paying jobs in the steel industry in Western Pennsylvania. Almost every family in town had three or four or five kids in it.

I hopped out of bed and opened the window. It was a perfect mid-June morning in my home town of Rockland. My backyard stretched out long and green in every direction until it melted into the neighbors' yards and then into their neighbors' yards and so on across the neighborhood, with only a dirt alleyway here and there to break up the sea of green. There were giant oaks and fruit trees and maple trees spread across the ball-field-sized yards. "I'll be out in ten minutes," I yelled down to my buddies. I could see they both had their bikes, with their baseball gloves hanging on the handle bars.

"Nelson, wake up," I said, shaking my brother's shoulder. "Looks like we're getting up a game."

"I'm not playing," my brother moaned as he pulled his sheets up over his head. "You go."

Nelson always disagreed with whatever I suggested, "Suit yourself," I shrugged, but five minutes later we were both in the kitchen wolfing down a bowl of Frosted Flakes. Harry and Sammy were already playing catch in my backyard.

"We're getting up a game, Mom," I told my mother as she tossed the bowls into the soapy gray water in the sink. She knew that was my way of asking if we could play in our yard.

"Why can't you play in Janie Kirkland's yard?" my mom complained. "Why does my yard always have to have those ugly bare spots all over it?" I had this conversation with my mother about fifty times each summer. I waited for the rest. "Besides, you'll break a window." She walked out of the kitchen and into the living room, where she was ironing clothes in front of the TV.

I knew my mom was right; we hosted more than our share of the neighborhood ball games. That was mostly because the other fathers in town worked shifts at the local steel mill. There was almost always somebody trying to get some sleep in the middle of the morning or afternoon. To wake up a sleeping father was unthinkable. Here was a man who left high school to defend his country, who came back to build the nation, who worked all night to feed his ever-growing family, who wanted nothing more than a hot meal and eight hours of sleep. It was *huge* deal to interrupt his sleep with noise from a pick-up game.

"Who the hell do these kids think they are?" one of the mill workers' wives would shout out over our heads at some invisible adult audience. "My husband worked eleven to seven last night. Why are they screaming and yelling while he's trying to get some sleep?"

We tried to stay away from sleeping fathers, but when we did happen to wake one up it was a bad situation. We knew all our neighbors personally. So our parents would get angry phone calls and we would all get punished. Everyone's parents doled out their own kind of punishment based on their nationality and whatever they learned in the army.

My dad worked for the same steel tube company as the other fathers, but he was an accountant and worked nine to five every day. That's why my mom would never strictly forbid us to play in our yard. She knew that sometimes it was our only option; she just made us feel guilty if we did.

I looked at Nelson and smiled. We both heard it. My mother never really said *no*. I waited until we were halfway out the door. "We won't break a window, we're using a rubber ball," I shouted down the hallway as we made our escape. I could hear her yelling something about going to the ball field as we ran out to join our buddies.

"How many do we got?" I asked as I took my place next to Harry and started warming up. We always used a regular hardball to loosen up, even though we used rubber balls for backyard games.

"Kenny's coming," Harry told me. "And the Dillons will be here as soon as they're done cleaning their room." Kenny was Harry's brother, only seven years old, but he could catch a ball and could even hit a little. Bo Dillon was my age, ten, and his brother Lonnie was nine. They always had to do chores in the morning before they were allowed to play ball.

"Go in and call Tony," Harry suggested. "That will give us eight. We can play with eight."

I hesitated to go back in the house. I knew my mother would tell us to take our game to the town's only real baseball field. She didn't understand the advantages of a backyard game.

It's not that we didn't like the Rockland ball field. That's where we played our Little League games and where we practiced with our organized teams. And it was only two blocks away. But it wasn't great for pick-up games. We could usually get eight to ten players from the neighborhood and you can't cover a regulation baseball diamond with only four or five guys on a team.

Besides, if the older kids showed up in the middle of our game, they would throw us off the field and take over. We didn't resent it. That's just the way it was. When we got older, we threw little kids off the field all the time.

Anyway, backyards were better for pick-up games. No one could throw you out of your own yard. Plus, there were houses and trees to knock down some of the fly balls. So you needed fewer players to cover the field. And our ground rules always said that a ball in a tree was *live*. If a fly ball went into a tree and bounced around the branches for a while, the fielders could still catch it and the batter was out.

It added a little drama and helped the fielders get some extra outs, so it shortened the games. And since we played backyard games with a rubber ball, there were almost no injuries.

"Why don't *you* call Tony?" I asked finally. Harry's house was just two doors away from mine. He could be there in thirty seconds. In fact our entire neighborhood was like one big yard. No one had fences or hedges. You could run a mile through the neighborhood and never hit a barrier. You were always in someone's backyard.

"I can't go back to my house," Harry said loud enough for only me to hear. "My mom walked down to my grandma's house and locked us out."

I guess he was embarrassed to admit that his mother had locked her kids out of the house, but Harry's grandmother only lived a block away and, if he needed anything, all the other mothers in the neighborhood would have been happy to help. Besides, I was glad to hear his mother was gone for a few hours. It meant we could start the game in *his* yard.

"Nobody has to call him," Sammy shouted as the ball smacked into his glove. "Here he comes." Tony came rattling in on his bike and skidded to a stop in the alleyway that bordered my yard. Of course his ball glove was hanging from the handlebar.

Tony was my cousin and best friend. He lived two blocks away, but he always came to our neighborhood to play ball. He was eleven, a year older than me, and was probably the best ballplayer in our group.

"Who else do we got?" Tony yelled as he flung his bike into the yard without putting down the kickstand. "Where's your rag?" he snapped at Nelson as he joined our game of catch. Tony called everybody's baseball glove their "rag." He wasn't trying to be insulting. He just acted like possessions meant nothing to him.

Tony's dad, my uncle Joe, was a pharmacist. He owned the town's only drugstore, one of the few retail businesses in Rockland. He earned quite a bit more money than the mill workers, but no one seemed to resent him for it. He was a good Italian boy who served his country in the biggest war of all time, came home and worked his way through school on the G.I. Bill, then came back to his hometown and opened his pharmacy.

Like all of us, Tony had a lot of siblings, two brothers and two sisters. But he always seemed to have better stuff than the rest of us. His bike was new, with a headlight he never lit and an electric horn he never honked. He always had new sneakers and a nice fielder's glove, *plus* a first baseman's mitt. His pockets were full of penny candy and new packs of baseball cards.

I always thought that Tony was the closest thing our town had to royalty. My big sister Sandy called him "Tony of the Drugstore."

He warded off jealously and resentment by showing his complete disregard for all material things.

"We got eight," I reported, "and Harry's mom just left to visit her mother and sisters."

My job was done. Tony had all the information he needed. Now all I had to do was wait for him to get the game started.

Tony was a born leader, and by that I mean he knew how to delegate. Most of us went along with whatever he suggested. Nelson, on the other hand, never went along with what anybody suggested. It was a recipe for disaster, and their personalities clashed every day.

Nelson paced back and forth under the back porch. "You don't have eight. You have seven. I'm not playing," he announced finally. "I don't feel like it."

"You're not playing?" Tony said sarcastically. "Everybody you know is playing. What are you going to do?" Nelson turned and walked slowly through our basement doorway.

"He's playing," Tony whispered to me as Nelson disappeared under the porch. I nodded my agreement.

The porch was big. It was attached to the house on one side and was supported by two big brick pillars on the other side. It sheltered an area large enough to park eight to ten bicycles comfortably. That made it the perfect rallying point for our crew, and most mornings started right here.

Nelson came out of the cellar a minute later with his glove and a shiny new blue rubber ball. I knew Nelson had bought the ball the day before. He spent ten cents on it that he could have otherwise used to buy two packs of baseball cards or ten pieces of licorice or two packs of sunflower seeds. Instead he invested in a new ball, so I knew he was going to play.

No one said a word to Nelson as he slowly and silently joined the warm-ups. Any sarcastic remarks at this point and our eighth player would be gone.

Over Harry's mild objections, we all left our bikes under the porch and started the short walk to his yard. "If your mom comes home, we'll leave," Tony coaxed him reassuringly. The Dillon boys appeared in the alleyway coming toward us from the other direction, and Harry's brother Kenny was already loosening up his arm by bouncing a rubber ball against the side of their brick ranch house, a sure sign that his mother wasn't home.

It was game time.

chapter three

I Know You

The echo of voices coming down the hall snapped me back to the fake leather chair in the corner of the pale-green hospital room. The noise drew closer and closer, a strange combination of laughter and moaning, of good-natured teasing and occasional shouts of anger.

Twenty years earlier, I had worked my way through college as a nurse's aide in the inpatient unit of a community mental health center, and the sound of inappropriate manic humor, short bursts of anguish from the depressives and wild ramblings of the schizophrenics triggered my old feelings of sympathy, frustration, and hopelessness. The sound was unmistakable; the mental patients were coming back from lunch.

I stepped out into the hallway to see if I could spot Harry. Immediately the din was reduced to a whisper as each patient, in turn, made eye contact with this stranger in the doorway. I tried to smile and nod a silent *hello*, tried to seem as nonthreatening as possible. Most of them smiled back, but no one spoke.

Then a toothless old man shouted, "Hey!" He was pointing at me. "Hey... hey," he stammered. His eyes were vacant and tired. His face was wrinkled and pale, but there was something familiar about it, like an old photograph of your dead great-grandfather. "Hey, I know you." His eyes opened wide then. "I *know* you."

"Oh my God," I murmured in disbelief, "it's Harry."

"I remember you. You're... you're Teddy Tresh!" The old man laughed in triumph. "I remember you. How come I remember you? I can't remember my son's name, but I remember you. You're Teddy Tresh."

"Harry, Harry," I trotted across the hall and grabbed him in a bear hug. There was morning mucous in his tear ducts and the corners of his toothless mouth were dry and crusty. "Harry, it's good to see you."

"I remember you," he rambled on, "I don't remember my kids' names, but I remember you."

"You've known me longer," I laughed. "You've known me all your life."

"Teddy Tresh," he repeated. "Teddy Tresh and… and Tony DeVito, you were my… my friends. I mean *were* you my friends?"

"Hell yes, we were your friends." I hugged him again. "We played ball and caught frogs and chased girls together. Look," I said and held out the team picture I had in my hand. "Here we are as kids. That's me right there … and that's you and this one's Tony DeVito."

Harry looked at the photo vacantly for a moment then tossed it on the bed. "Teddy Tresh," he stated proudly. "Teddy Tresh and Tony DeVito… my friends. How come I know you?"

I reached over and picked the framed newspaper picture off his blanket and ceremoniously placed it on his windowsill. The sun shining through the bars cast an ominous striped shadow across the players' faces. "Sit down," I said, "I'll tell you all about it."

Janie Kirkland had warned that Harry might not recognize me, so his reaction was a bonus; but now I wondered how much more of my friend was left inside this scary-looking old man. He was only forty-five years old. What the hell had happened to him to make him look like this?

Then I remembered a phone conversation I had had with Tony just a week before. "You're going to see Harry?" he had asked. He cautioned me, "You won't recognize him. His mother tried to bring him home about eight years ago. He wandered out of the house one day and went straight into a bar. He was mumbling so bad no one could understand a word he was saying. Then he reached out and grabbed some woman's ass and her husband knocked his front teeth out. They sent him straight back to Mayview. His brain was so screwed up, nobody paid attention to his teeth. Eventually they all rotted and had to be pulled out. He's a mess, Teddy."

"Do you want to go with me?" I had hoped Tony would share my burden of visiting Harry in this mental institution. My family and I had moved to Boston fifteen years earlier, shortly after Harry's attack of viral encephalitis, but now we were back in the Pittsburgh area and I was determined to pay him a long overdue visit.

"I *should* go, Teddy." His voice had been suddenly solemn and defensive. "But I've been there once before and I just can't go back… I can't." His soft words had sent shivers down my spine. I never thought Tony was afraid of anything.

Then he made it worse. "Sure, he was our best friend when we were kids. But when he got older, he only cared about himself." I knew Tony was making excuses for his own fears and doubts, but everything he said was true. When Harry was in his twenties, with a wife and two kids, he still chased women around. And he borrowed money from everyone he knew, never intending to pay it back.

"When he had the attack," Tony had confided, "he owed me a figure close to five dimes. That's five thousand I'll never see again."

"But he was our best pal," I had tried to persuade him.

"I know he was, Teddy." His voice had been barely audible. "But I just can't go back. I'm sorry."

So now I stood here alone in this terrible place, facing a broken, brain-damaged old shell of a man. Was there any piece of my childhood friend still in there? "Do you remember the trestle?" I asked Harry finally. "And playing 'Release' in the neighborhood? And the baseball games? My God, we played ball every day of the summer!"

Now Harry looked at me blankly and I could see the fear and frustration building in his ancient eyes. "I remember the woods," he said finally, "and the railroad tracks." It was coming back in bits and pieces now. "And the yards!" His excitement was starting to build. "We all had big yards!"

"That's right," I said, "and you had the best yard of all." And as I started speaking I could see it, the green of the grass and shadows from the trees; I could feel the heat of the sun and the coolness of the shade. I had forgotten too. Forgotten the joy.

chapter four

Whole Hands or Nothing

Harry's yard was perfectly laid out for a ball field. The ground was smooth and the grass was plush. There was a thirty-foot-high maple tree just behind third base. Beyond the tree, the yard was wide open for about two hundred feet then emptied into Connie Pinchotti's yard on the other side of the alley.

Connie was one of three beautiful little ten-year-old girls who lived in my neighborhood. The other two were Linda—Harry's sister—and Stephanie—Sammy's sister. "There's no beauty like an Italian beauty," my Serbian-Irish father used to tell me. And that's the only explanation I could ever find for how three little girls that gorgeous could grow up together in one tiny neighborhood.

Connie was one of the rarest types of children in Rockland. She was an only child. Everyone else I knew had at least two siblings. She was also my second cousin. In that respect, she was not unique. There were about 900 people living in the entire town of Rockland; nearly 200 of them were relatives of mine.

My mother's side of the family was second- and third-generation Italian-American. Her grandparents were Italian stonecutters who had come to Rockland around 1900 to work in the town's vast stone quarry. The first generation had twelve kids and the second generation had fourteen more, so a big chunk of Rockland was my family.

The entire town was made up of grandsons and granddaughters of immigrants, mostly Italian immigrants. Harry and I were half Italian. Our fathers came home after the war, married little Italian girls from Rockland and settled down to work at the local steel mill.

The Bellissimos and the Pinchottis were full-blooded Italians. They had suffered through the Great Depression and the closing of the stone quarries. They had been the victims of poverty and prejudice throughout their young lives. But now they were war heroes, returning to their little hometown to buy houses and work the booming post-war steel industry. Although it never completely returned to its years of prosperity when slate and stone were the building blocks of America, Rockland was still their kingdom. And, even though some folks in the surrounding communities looked down their noses at the small immigrant steel town, Rockland was still their promised land.

I could see Connie's little suntanned face looking out her bedroom window as we prepared to start the game. Stephanie and Linda were both with her and they took turns peering out at us, waiting until just the right moment to make their entrance. Sometimes, when we couldn't get enough guys for a decent game, we would ask the girls to play. Of course, that changed the complexion of the ballgame completely. All three of them were terrible ball players. Linda could catch and hit a little, but Stephanie and Connie couldn't catch at all and struck out most of the time. I was hoping they wouldn't ask to play today. I preferred it when they were just spectators.

In right-center field, just behind the second baseman, was a row of six ten-foot pine trees. Between the pines Harry's mother always had flowers growing. Some years she planted marigolds, some years impatiens, and this year pansies. We had to be extremely careful not to stomp the flowers. Janie Kirkland took tremendous pride in her gardening. She was another local Italian girl who married a veteran and settled right back into her hometown, where she was raising four kids. Her crowning glories were her shrubbery and her flower beds. A crushed or broken flower meant we would be banished from Harry's yard for at least two weeks.

There was an open space of grass behind the pine trees, then a fairly large cornfield. The cornfield was owned and tended by Harry's maternal grandfather, Nick Fratelli. He was probably about sixty years old, but he looked eighty. He walked down the alleyway every morning, pushing an old wheelbarrow full of garden tools. His back was rounded with age and his fingers were bent and arthritic with dirt permanently ground into the pores and fingernails. He would stop and smile and wave. And we would all chuckle at the way he swung his arms and carried on long, loud, animated Italian conversations with some invisible companion walking beside him.

"I think he's talking to God," I once told Harry. "Nah, he's just screaming at my grandmother," Harry shrugged. "Something he wouldn't dare do to her face." Harry always seemed embarrassed by the way his grandmother dominated her husband, but old man Fratelli always seemed happy to me, working two big gardens on his property, growing the biggest, best-tasting vegetables in town.

Just like the flowers, any broken cornstalks meant banishment from the yard. Therefore, any ball hit into the cornfield was an automatic double.

We laid out the bases. Two red bricks laid side-by-side served as first, second, and third base. Home plate was a pizza box from somebody's trash can.

Harry, who was twelve years old, and Tony, eleven, were the oldest, so they *picked-up,* that is, they chose the teams.

Harry picked up one of the three wooden bats we had for the game and flipped it toward Tony. "Whole hands or nothing," he called out. "Winner gets the first pick, loser gets the next two." They alternated hand-over-hand up toward the knob at the end of the handle. Tony got the last full hand.

"I'll take Teddy," he called out. Now Harry got the next two picks. "Sammy and Bo," he said quickly.

Tony hesitated. I knew why. My brother Nelson was a little better than Lonnie Dillon. But Nelson was always a threat to quit in the middle of the game, especially if a call went against him or if he were playing poorly or even if he just got bored. "I'll take Nelson," Tony said finally. Nelson gave him a dirty look as he walked over and stood between us. I could tell he resented the hesitation. "Lonnie," Harry said with his final pick. "And we'll take Kenny," Tony replied. Kenny was Harry's brother, but he was only seven years old and didn't mind being the last pick. He was just happy to be playing.

The three girls made their entrance just as the game was about to begin. They sat on the hillside in foul territory along the third baseline, chatting and giggling in those high-pitched voices that all beautiful little girls seem to have. Harry's sister, Linda, spoke first. "Can we play?" Linda was the most outgoing of the three, but they were all pleasant and easy to talk to.

"No," Harry snapped, "We already have our teams."

"But stick around," I added quickly, "in case somebody has to leave." They all smiled and shook their heads. Although I was only ten years old and heading into fifth grade, most of my best friends were seventh-graders. Even Tony, who was only eleven, had started school early and was already heading into seventh grade. I always tried my best to be like Tony, so I was already pretty good at talking to girls. "Wait your turn, ladies," Tony taunted with a wink as he pulled down on the brim of his red baseball hat. "You'll get your chance."

Nelson and the younger kids didn't have much interest in girls. They would just as soon be catching frogs as flirting with Stephanie, Connie, and Linda. But Harry, Tony, and I were following some unexplainable need to make a girl's eyes light up. Just like baseball, it was a skill we were honing for the future. As for the girls... well, they were only ten. But they always seemed years ahead of us in maturity and flirting was almost second nature to them.

The action started quickly as we put up six runs in the top of the first. We would have scored more, but the inning ended on a bizarre play.

With two outs, I was standing on first base after a two-run single when Nelson hit a high pop-up into the maple tree behind third base. Lonnie, who was playing left-center field, came charging in to try to make the play. Meanwhile, Harry, who was at shortstop, also tried to get under the ball, which was now bouncing around in the upper branches of the tree. Both players tried to follow the ball and Harry finally called out, "I got it."

It looked like a sure out, but just eight feet off the ground, the rubber ball tipped one last branch and hit Harry on the top of the head. With two outs, I was running at the crack of the bat. I had already touched second and was on my way to third when I saw the ball bop off Harry's head. So I kept going. Meanwhile, the girls, sitting just a few feet away, burst into that high-pitched, contagious giggling that's irresistible to preteen boys.

As luck would have it, the ball bounced off Harry's head and went directly to Tony, who was acting as courtesy catcher. He caught the ricochet and tagged me out at the plate as Harry spun around and around still looking for the ball. The inning was over.

When we took the field, Kenny went to first base. I went to the shortstop third-base area. Tony would roam the entire outfield while Nelson went out to pitch. The team who was batting would provide a courtesy catcher to the team in the field.

The courtesy catcher was expected to catch pop fouls and cover home plate, putting out his own teammates. To their credit, these catchers were amazingly honest. Sure, there was the occasional dropped pop-up or bobbled play at the plate. But no one intentionally dropped the ball. I'm not sure why.

With only four fielders, our defense had to be amoeba-like, changing with every batter and every situation. With a runner at first base, our first baseman would move over to cover second base to get the forced out there. If a "little guy" came to bat, we might put all our fielders into the infield and dare him to hit it over our heads.

This particular game was a high-scoring affair. Even little Kenny was putting the ball in play. And in the top of the sixth and final inning, we came to bat with a 16–10 lead.

On the first pitch of the inning, Tony hit a line drive into one of the ten-foot pines behind second base. The ball stuck in the tree and Bo jumped into the pine needles to retrieve it. He pulled the ball out as Tony headed for second. Bo ran five steps and dove to make the tag on Tony, sliding into the base. "Safe," I yelled at the top of my lungs.

"Out! He was out," screamed Bo. He completely ignored Tony, who was still lying in the grass with his feet on the two red bricks and his arms extended in the *safe* signal, and charged straight for me. We all argued with each other at every game. Arguments usually took up about ten to twenty percent of our game time. But Bo wasn't good at arguments; he usually came out swinging. And although I was still shouting about Tony's foot getting under the glove, Bo had stopped arguing and had now thrown off his glove and had both his hands balled into fists.

I hated getting punched by Bo Dillon's sledgehammer hands, so I decided to tackle him and turn it into a wrestling match. I was the better wrestler, probably because my brother and I wrestled every single day.

I lowered my shoulder as I raced toward him trying to build momentum, when all at once we heard Harry wailing, "The flowers! You stomped my mother's flowers!"

Everyone froze in fear as thoughts of parental punishment blocked out all other matters. We ran to the flowerbed between the pines for a closer look. There they were. Three purple pansies crushed beyond recognition. Harry was kneeling over them, hopelessly trying to prop up the petals that just kept flopping pathetically back to the ground.

We all looked at each other in silence for a few seconds. And then, as if someone had fired a gun to start the Boston Marathon, we all broke into a sprint across the grass, grabbing bats and gloves and balls as we went. The girls ran straight for the sanctuary of Connie's house. Only Harry stayed behind, trying to play Jesus to the lepers in the flowerbed.

The rest of us looked like greyhounds chasing a rabbit, jostling, jumping over hedges, pushing each other out of the way, falling to the ground, rolling over to our feet, across Harry's well-groomed lawn, through the neighbor's yard, into my yard and under my porch. Then we hopped on our bikes and rode down the alleyway toward the drugstore. We would regroup there, wonder about the repercussions of the great flower stomping and even argue about who had won the game.

It was as if there were no tomorrow, just as it should have been, just as it always should be.

chapter five

Swiss Cheese

Harry was laughing now, the first sign of any joy I had seen on his face in fifteen years. Although the sun was shining brilliantly through the windows, his little green room had seemed drab and hopeless and surrounded by the fog of mental illness. But now some brightness seemed to filter into the place. Tony had told me that Harry's brain was like Swiss cheese, but here was a glimmer of hope.

"So you remember the pansies!" I said, placing a hand on Harry's shoulder as his high-pitched laughter filled the air.

"No," he replied after catching his breath. "I don't know what you're talking about."

Now I cracked up and burst into peals of laughter, which only escalated Harry's mood. His eyes were practically closed as he roared in amusement. It brought patients and nurses to his doorway and tears to his eyes. "Is everything okay in here?" the pastel RN asked in her controlled voice, still smiling like a small child waiting for the photographer to snap her picture.

"Everything's fine," I gasped between breaths as both Harry and I tried to regain our composure. Of course that only made the outburst harder to control. And we continued to chuckle and snicker off and on as the motionless nurse with her dead eyes and gargoyle smile watched us for another two minutes without uttering a word. She was obviously upset by the disruption we had caused on her ward but wasn't exactly sure how to handle it.

Finally she turned on Harry. "How about taking a shower for me today, Mr. Kirkland?" She looked at him condescendingly. "You haven't showered since Sunday."

I hate mental wards, I thought.

Finally she withdrew from the doorway and I turned my attention back to Harry. I noticed there were still tears in his eyes and a long-forgotten memory came rushing back. Harry had always laughed until he cried. We used to tease him about it. It got to the point where he would cover his eyes to avoid detection. And a joke or a ridiculous situation wasn't considered funny unless it made Harry cry.

"So you *don't* remember your mother's flowers?" I asked as though the interruption had never occurred. "Do you remember the ball games? The arguments? The bikes?"

"No." He nodded as his smile slowly faded away. "What about the girls?" I asked.

"Stephanie, Connie, and Linda," he beamed back proudly. I wasn't really surprised that he knew those names. After all, Linda was his sister and Stephanie and Connie were her constant companions.

They were together so often that their three names became like one name. "Who's coming down the street?" Stephanie, Connie, and Linda. "Who's having a cookout?" Stephanie, Connie and Linda. "Who wants to go swimming?" Stephanie, Connie, and Linda. It became a mantra, a chant. Hell, it was almost poetic.

I was happy Harry remembered the names, but not excited. How could he forget that? It would be like Pavlov's dog forgetting to salivate.

"Can you think of anything else?" I offered hopefully.

His eyes lit up. "I remember the drugstore."

"Wow," I said, "that's great!" And it was great. Not only was he still aware of our favorite childhood hangout, but it fit right into the context of the story I was telling him. This was significant. This was beyond my expectations. I wasn't just fulfilling a long-overdue obligation to call on a sick friend; I might actually enjoy this visit.

Before the moment could get away, I launched back into that summer.

chapter six

Does That Hurt?

We all pulled our bikes up to the front of DeVito's Drugstore and screeched to a stop. Most bikes had coaster brakes in those days. Coaster brakes were absolute. They stopped the back wheel dead as soon as you pushed back on the pedal, and we would leave beautiful black skid marks on the sidewalk as we hopped off our bikes and threw down the kickstands all in one motion.

Of course, the catch was that the bike could have only one speed. Once more people started buying three-speed, five-speed and ten-speed bikes, they needed to pedal backwards to change gears, so coaster brakes became less and less popular. Like nurses' white uniforms, it's just one more thing that didn't need to change.

Inside my uncle Joe's drugstore was a soda fountain with eight round stools at the counter. The green stools could swivel around 360 degrees, but they never seemed to wear out. They never even wobbled.

The counter had a yellow Formica top with a pattern of little blue ovals all over it. The underside of the counter, for the few of us who ever looked at it, was covered with disgusting wads of dried-up chewing gum that people would stick there when their sodas arrived. There were hundreds and hundreds of wads of gum under the counter. In fact, 10,000 years from now, if anthropologists ever dig up that store and find that counter, they could easily clone the entire population of Rockland circa 1964.

Seven of us pulled up outside the drugstore that day and tried to compose ourselves before going in. Uncle Joe could sniff out guilt a mile away, and if we came into the store giggling and smirking, he would have questioned us like the Nazis at Nuremberg.

We walked up to the counter and ordered our favorite sodas. Mine was cherry Coke, which was a regular fountain Coke with cherry syrup added. "Ten cents apiece, boys," my uncle said matter-of-factly, giving me a quick wink. Of course, we all knew Tony didn't have to pay for his soda. It was his dad's store.

I pulled a quarter out of my pocket. "This is for me and Nelson," I proclaimed loudly enough for everyone to hear.

"Thank you," nodded Uncle Joe as he handed me my change, two dimes and a nickel. This was a little charade we played any time my buddies were with me. Everyone expected Tony to drink for free, but Nelson and I were nephews. If we got ours for free, it might cause some hard feelings among the other families in the neighborhood. Of course, we weren't regular nephews; we were his only sister's only sons. But other people still might resent it.

I understood that my uncle had to draw the line somewhere. He was related to nearly 200 people in town, and almost every person in Rockland considered themselves to be his close friends. They called him Jiggy, a nickname he picked up in childhood for no apparent reason. The older folks treated him like a son. The other grown-ups treated him like a brother. The kids all treated him like a baseball coach, because at one time or another he had hit ground balls and thrown batting practice to practically every kid in town. If his drugstore didn't charge family and friends, he'd go broke.

We all sat at the counter as "Jiggy" went into the back room to fill prescriptions. "It was only a six-inning game," Tony finally offered, "and we were up by six runs in the last inning. It's just like a rainout. We win the game." Bo disagreed, but "Huhh!" was all he said. "Sure," I continued, "it's a complete game after four innings, just like a rainout."

It was amazing how seriously we took these daily pick-up games. It was all an illusion, of course. Each day's game was played, then forgotten, like a giant Etch-a-Sketch.

Just then we heard another bike screech to a stop outside and in walked Harry. The place fell suddenly quiet. "How bad is it?" Tony whispered sympathetically.

"My mother's going to kill me!" Harry barked at all of us. Of course, Janie Kirkland was a screamer, not a hitter. But she was the best in Rockland. She would yell at her kids for weeks over an offense like this. Then, when she told our parents, as we knew she would, we would all catch a little hell for it. "Poor Harry," I thought. When my dad found out, he would give me and Nelson a couple whacks on the butt and it would be over. But Harry would have to put up with the insults and anger for hours. "I'd rather have the whacks," I whispered to Nelson.

Looking down the counter, I could see we were all contemplating our punishments. Nelson and I would get spanked with a belt across our behinds. Sammy and the Dillon boys would get grounded for a few days, doing hard time in their fathers' gardens. My uncle Joe would roar at Tony and threaten him for about five minutes, then never bring it up again.

Our mothers would all be embarrassed and scream at us, except for Tony's mom, my Aunt Betty, who would pretend to be embarrassed and pretend to be angry with him. But she would really be thinking, "Who gives a shit? They're just flowers."

All the same, we dreaded being punished. "Maybe she won't find out?" Nelson offered in a loud whisper.

"Of course she'll find out," muttered Sammy, "there are three dead flowers laying there."

"No there aren't," Harry sighed as he laid the three crushed and shriveled pansies on the counter. "I pulled them out."

"She'll see the bare spots," Tony jumped in. "Maybe not," said Harry hopefully, "I got a shovel and moved some of them around. Then I watered them all."

"What're the chances she won't notice?" I was still whispering so as not to attract the attention of my uncle. "About three-to-two," Tony laughed. Even at the age of eleven he was pretty good at judging probability, a quality he would master in later life. I was relieved. A few minutes earlier, I was thinking that punishment was inevitable. Now I had a forty-percent chance of getting off scot-free. I decided to file this under "things I can worry about tomorrow" and put it out of my mind.

Besides, my uncle was about to say something that would make me forget all about some broken flowers. "We've got Steve's Barbershop tonight," his voice boomed from the back room from among thousands of pill bottles, ointments, and other assorted tools of his trade.

Steve's Barbershop was the sponsor of one of the four organized Little League teams in our town. The others were McDowell's Hotel, the Boosters, and the Board of Trade.

Tony, Harry, and I played for the Board of Trade and Uncle Joe was our coach. "Who are they throwing?" I asked sheepishly.

"Who do you think?!!" my uncle's voice boomed back.

Again, the entire store fell silent. A visitor from another city or state or country would have been shocked at the immediate effect my uncle's words had on the counter full of happy young boys sitting on those stools. Our eyes popped wide open, our lips pulled tight against our teeth. We looked at one another in fear and dread.

"Who do you think?" the question hung in the air like a stick of dynamite just after the fuse stops hissing and just before the boom. We all knew the answer: Dawson!

Derrick Dawson was just twelve years old but was already nearly six feet tall. His fastball exploded. His left-handed curveball broke so sharply that it often sent left-handed batters sprawling to the ground just before it broke across the inside corner for a called strike. And the worst part of it all was that he had perfect control of both pitches.

He was scary fast, plus he knew how to pitch. He knew when to work the corners and when to bust a pitch inside. When the batter was completely overmatched, Dawson knew when to just blow it past him. Quite simply, he was the best Little League pitcher I had ever seen or ever will see. Even today, when I watch the Little League World Series on TV and see these teams from Taiwan or Japan dominating the American teams, I think, "They would have never hit Dawson."

Only Nelson and Lonnie were smiling. Like the big left-hander, they both played for Steve's Barbershop. Bo played for McDowell's and Sammy played for the Boosters. They both looked intently at their sodas. They didn't say a word, but I knew what they were thinking. If we were getting Dawson tonight, then their team wouldn't have to face him later in the week.

Finally, Sammy spoke. "He's not unhittable."

It almost seemed funny to hear him say it. Sammy was a big kid for an eight-year-old, but he was just an eight-year-old. In most of the cities and towns in Western Pennsylvania, eleven- and twelve-year-olds would have had their own

Little League, while the younger kids would still be in Farm League. But our town was so small that in order to fill the rosters for four teams, the league grouped together all kids aged eight through twelve. Each team carried about thirteen or fourteen players.

It was important to the town to have its own Little League, even if they did have to have second-graders playing against seventh-graders. It showed independence and pride and I always sensed that there was some resentment among the Rockland fathers that when they were kids, they had not been treated fairly when it came to playing ball in some of the bigger towns in the area.

They were the sons of immigrants, struggling to get through the Depression, and they were pretty sure this had hurt their opportunities, especially when it came to sports. With their own league, no outsider could limit their sons' playing time; no big-town umpire could slant the calls against their boys.

Still, seeing any eight-year-old trying to bat against any twelve-year-old pitcher was a pretty sad sight. Seeing an eight-year-old trying to hit Dawson was just ridiculous.

"He's right!" my uncle said, blasting back into the room, his hands full of freshly filled prescription bottles. "This little kid's got more guts than the rest of you put together."

"Just throw your hands, goddamn it." He was at full volume now. "Here," he screamed, laying one of the plastic pill bottles on the counter, then swatting it across the room with a smooth swipe of his wrist. "Here," he shouted again, repeating the action. "Just turn your wrists. Trust your swing, for Chrissakes." My uncle had spent hundreds of hours in the batting cage with every kid sitting at that counter. The fact that we considered Dawson unbeatable was more than he could stand.

"I'm not afraid of him," I said finally. It was sort of a lie, I guess. What I really meant was that I wasn't as afraid of Dawson as I was of my uncle Joe. Looking back on it across the years, I think that's the effect he was hoping to have on us.

Baseball, especially for Little Leaguers, is about overcoming your fear of the hard ball. It's not easy to concentrate on your swing with a seventy-mile-an-hour missile coming at you from forty-six feet away.

Tony left his head down an instant too long. "What's the worst that could happen?" His dad now turned on him. "You get hit with a pitch?"

"So what? So what?" his dad continued raving. "I've got news for all of you. If you want to play this game you *are* going to get hit." Now he noticed the bag of warm-up balls he had stored behind the counter. "Here," he shouted, grabbing a baseball in his hand and pounding it against Tony's chest. "Here," he screamed again, pounding it against my chest. "Does that hurt?"

"No," we replied in unison. "Dawson's not going to hit you any harder than that," he shouted. "I guarantee you!" And with that he stormed off to the back room again, first stopping to pick up and examine the two pill bottles lying in the aisle.

I looked up and down the counter. There were seven of us still seated. Somehow Harry, who never got the chance to order his Coke, had snuck out the door during my uncle's tirade. When the rest of us got outside, there was Harry sitting on his bike smirking at us. "Boy, I saw that one coming," he chuckled. "When Jiggy's on the warpath you gotta move fast."

"You still have to face your mother," Tony warned, as the smile ran away from Harry's face.

I was back on my bike now, straddling the seat and rubbing my chest. Finally, I pulled up my jersey to examine the spot where Dawson's simulated "pitch" had hit me. It was blue and red and I could easily make out the stitches of a baseball imprinted on my skin. "Damn it," I said, "your old man's nuts."

"Shit," added Tony, as he examined his own purple chest. "I have to pitch tonight."

"That doesn't hurt, does it?" chimed in my brother, Nelson, as he mockingly slapped at my bruise. "That doesn't hurt," he said, slapping again. "No," I replied. "And *this* doesn't hurt either." I punched him in the shoulder. Soon we were rolling around on the sidewalk wrestling. It was our first fight of the day. My brother and I averaged about three fights per day. He started all of them, but I was happy to oblige. If my mother saw us, she would tell my dad when he came home and we'd get whacked with the belt about three times a week.

"Save your strength, you two," Sammy intervened, "you've got a real game tonight."

Slowly I let my brother up from the pavement. "At least I don't have to face Dawson," he taunted, as he gave me one final push.

"You have to face me," Tony replied, "and my control's not nearly as good as Dawson's."

Now we all headed our separate ways. Tony's house was right above the drugstore, so he just walked up the steps. Nelson and I went home for lunch and to rest up for the game. Sammy had to do some work in his father's garden and Bo and Lonnie still had more chores to do.

Harry and Kenny stopped at their grandmother's house to grab a sandwich and to make sure that their mother was still visiting. Their plan was to stall as long as possible, to keep their mother there until the newly watered flowers had time to dry.

By four that afternoon, I hadn't heard any screaming from the Kirklands' house, so I figured we were in the clear. Nelson and I had a quick bowl of soup for dinner and then headed upstairs to put on our uniforms. Game time was six o'clock and we had to be at the field by five. Nelson was still laughing and trying to goad me into another wrestling match, but my thoughts were fixated on one thing—Derrick Dawson.

chapter seven

A Slice of Pride

"Dawson." Harry's old eyes sharpened with recognition. His brow furrowed. His head nodded slowly. Fear and respect flashed across his toothless, wrinkled face. "Dawson," he repeated. Brain damage or no brain damage, Harry's reaction was spot on.

"What do you remember about him?" I asked.

"He was mean," said Harry.

Wrong. Derrick Dawson wasn't mean. His curveball was mean. His fastball was scary. But the kid himself wasn't mean. He had sleepy eyes and he almost seemed to be emotionless. No highs and lows, no excitement or frustration, no fear or anger. It made him an even better pitcher because nothing seemed to rattle him.

"Was he on our team?" Harry asked.

"Sometimes he was, sometimes he wasn't," I replied. "During the regular season we had to bat against him. During the all-star season he pitched for us."

Harry looked confused. How could I remind him what it was like to face the six-foot lefty with the blazing fastball and knee-buckling curve? And then describe what it felt like to play behind him, when every batter was a potential strike-out victim and those who didn't strike out would hit the ball feebly to the opposite field?

"Remember, Harry, we played right-hand batters to hit to the right side and left-hand batters to hit to left." I thought this might bring a flicker of recognition to Harry's rattled memory. After all, this was just the opposite of how we played behind any other pitcher.

"You were our shortstop." I continued. "And I played second base."

"I *was* the shortstop," Harry announced proudly. "Not Ray Marino, not Teddy Tresh, me… I was the shortstop."

I was stunned by the comment. It was way beyond the limits of what they told me Harry was capable of understanding. Ray Marino was the third baseman for our Little League all-star team in 1964, but in later years he would become one of the finest shortstops in the town's history. I was our ten-year-old second baseman, two years behind Ray and Harry, but I would go on to play shortstop for the Rockland Little League, Pony League, Colt League and American Legion teams for the next eight years.

Although I probably grew nine inches in the next three years, and Ray got stronger and bigger season after season, Harry never seemed to grow much after 1964. He really peaked at a very early age. When we hit our teenage years, I always felt he kind of resented me for it. Was he a better shortstop than I was? Better than Ray was? Yes, that year he was better.

But how could Harry and his five-year-old intellect possibly comprehend this level of irony?

"You remember Ray Marino?" I asked him.

"Who?"

"Ray Marino," I repeated. "You just mentioned him!"

Harry looked away, disturbed at the holes in his short-term memory.

"You *just* said his name," I blurted. But whatever spark of memory or slice of self-esteem that had evoked his comment was gone.

"Tell me about Dawson," Harry said. "Was he really unhittable?"

The question brought back a wave of memories and emotions. I could see the big left-hander on the mound, fierce and confident. "Nobody's unhittable," I said finally, "but he was pretty close."

chapter eight

The Real Games

The baseball field was a short four-minute walk from my house. It was down on Sixth Avenue, the easternmost road in Rockland. It bordered Babcock & Wilcox, a huge steel mill that employed about half the fathers in town. In fact, the B & W's chain-link security fence that surrounded the steel yard also served as our right field wall.

One of the factory buildings just beyond the fence had a huge forty-foot square door that was always open. Every hour or so a gigantic bucket hanging from a crane would appear at the door and pour orange-hot molten steel into eight-ton molds. The liquid fire would crackle and boom as it hit the cooler molds and sparks would fly out the door and into the air. At night it looked like fireworks, lighting up the evening sky behind right field. Even during the day, it sounded like a huge thunderstorm. But nobody ever complained about the noise. Nobody ever complained about the smoky air. Nobody ever complained about the steel mill at all. It was the goose that laid the golden egg, the source of our wonderful lives.

Sometimes during ball games the umpires would call time-out until the roar of the molten steel hitting the molds subsided enough that we could hear each other's voices again. It was quite a show, I guess, but we were so used to it that we hardly even noticed.

Although the fence surrounding the company's property formed our right-field wall, there was no wall in left field or center field. So any ball hit over the outfielders' heads would just keep rolling.

Nelson and I arrived at the field about five o'clock. Our uniforms were identical white wool pants and tops with different color trims and sponsor names in script across the chest. Nelson's Steve's Barbershop uniform was trimmed in royal blue stripes and letters. My Board of Trade uniform was trimmed in red.

There was a big controversy in my family when my uncle Joe failed to pick Nelson in the first round of the Little League draft. About a dozen eight- and nine-year-olds were needed to fill out the Little League rosters that year, and Nelson was probably about the fifth-best player available. The Board of Trade had the first pick and took a kid named Sonny DeVito. He had the same last name as Tony and Uncle Joe but, amazingly, his family was not related to us. Still, they were Italians, and Jiggy almost always drafted Italians.

Sonny was a good little infielder and Uncle Joe was hoping to take him with his first-round pick and still be able to get Nelson in the second round. But Tony and I were pretty good Little League players from a family of good ballplayers. The gene pool for Nelson was considered pretty strong. Steve's Barbershop took him with their first-round pick.

My dad was furious. He knew Tony and I were close friends and that playing for Uncle Joe's team made us even closer. He also knew that my uncle always demanded dedication from his players. We were the hardest-working, best-trained team in the league. No one ever looked down their noses at the boys on the Board of Trade. We just exuded confidence and pride. That's what he wanted for Nelson, to be part of the *family* team. It sounds like a small problem, but it was a major source of tension in our family for years.

I walked over to the home-team dugout, along the first base line, while Nelson joined his team warming up in left field. I could see Dawson tossing softly with "Beans" Baruby, the Steve's Barbershop catcher.

His real name was Don Baruby, but apparently he had been a colicky baby, and his resulting "stomach noises" led his father to comment, "You're feeding that kid too many beans." It was a joke, of course, but it became so familiar that all his dad had to say was "beans" every time the kid burped or farted and everyone in the room would crack up. Eventually, *everyone* started calling him "Beans." It sounds like a degrading name, but he never seemed to mind it at all. In fact, he may have been the happiest kid I ever knew.

We took five or six rounds of infield with Uncle Joe barking instructions like a drill sergeant and hitting ground balls at us as hard as he could. The Board of Trade had the best infield in the league, and it was all because of Uncle Joe's demanding style.

Soon, we were working so hard at knocking down the ball and whipping it around the bases that we forgot all about the dominant pitcher we would soon be facing. There's no time to worry about Dawson's fastball when the next ground ball off Jiggy's bat could kill you.

The spectators started arriving, including my parents, the neighborhood girls, and my girlfriend, Molly Belinsky. I know I said I used to chat up the neighborhood girls every day. But Molly was my first real girlfriend. I saw Stephanie, Connie, and Linda 365 days a year. They would become my lifelong friends, but I was never really *boyfriend and girlfriend* with any of them.

Molly was different. She lived way up on Second Avenue, all the way across town. We went to grade school together, but I didn't really know her that well. She was cute and sweet and had long brown hair that was silky and soft. She was tiny, the smallest girl in our class, and I was the tallest boy in class.

Was I ready for a steady girl at age ten? Probably not. Was she ready for a boyfriend? The girls always seemed years ahead of us in maturity. She was ready.

I remember my first, clumsy attempts at courting her. I had a habit of arriving at St. Teresa's School just before the bell rang. I'd run into the cloakroom at the last second, hang up my jacket on a hook, and put my book bag on the top shelf. Then I would notice Molly's book bag on the floor under her coat. I would grab her bag and toss it up next to mine.

There weren't many boys in the fourth grade that had any interest in girls, but there was no use taking any chances. The only one in class who could reach her book bag at that height was me. I was her hero at least twice a day. Besides, like I said, I was pretty good at talking to girls. I was also motivated by the fact that my cousin Tony was going with Molly's cousin, Pam Genova. If Tony had a girlfriend, I figured I should have one too.

At game time, there were maybe eighty to a hundred fans on hand, mostly close friends and relatives, but to us it was like a World Series game. Tony pitched great that night and had given up only one run in the first five innings of the six-inning game, but Dawson was Dawson and when we came to bat in the bottom of the fifth, we still hadn't had even one base runner.

Tony was our left-handed cleanup hitter and started off the inning with a bloop single to left field, our first hit. Harry, batting fifth in the lineup, tried to bunt Tony over to second, but instead popped the bunt up in the air. Beans grabbed it for the first out.

Now, I stepped to the plate and looked down to Uncle Joe, who was coaching at third. To my horror, he was flashing me the *take* sign. Dawson had blown me out on three pitches in my first at-bat, with two outside corner fastballs and a big breaking pitch that made me look silly. But had my uncle lost so much faith in me that he wasn't even going to let me swing?

Then I saw it: the *steal* signal. He wanted me to take a pitch to allow Tony time to steal second base and get into scoring position. Tony was fast, but there was no guarantee he would be successful. Beans had the best arm in the league. But the pitch was a little low and the catcher's off-balance throw bounced into second base where the shortstop, Walt Terry, couldn't handle it. Tony was safe at second and our team, which had been quiet for so long, suddenly burst to life.

The pitch had been just outside the strike zone and Dawson, who was normally so reserved, seemed pissed off that he didn't get the call. He was also aggravated that his shortstop didn't hold the catcher's throw, and he glared at Walt, who just hung his head in dismay.

I was one of the better ten-year-old hitters in the league, but I was no match for Dawson at his best. Still, if he made a mistake, I had a chance.

In my first at-bat I had looked pathetic, and the big left-hander now decided to forget about nibbling at the corners and just blow me away with fastballs down the middle.

He reached back and fired. I fought back my fear, threw my hands, turned my wrists, and trusted my swing, just like Uncle Joe had loudly instructed that afternoon. I caught the pitch right on the nose and lined it past the mound and up the middle. Tony was digging for the plate and their centerfielder was charging hard to make the throw home.

There was only one problem; the Steve's Barbershop coach had substituted his regular centerfielder, the strong-armed Ricky Baldwin, with his own tiny eight-year-old son, Jerry Campbell. In his defense, Little League rules dictated

chapter nine

Do You Know Who You Are?

"Rockland boy to Rockland boy," Harry repeated, as he looked out through the bars of his hospital window onto the grounds of the institution, with its neatly trimmed lawns and hedges. "Rockland boy to Rockland boy." He spun around and faced me. "*I'm* a Rockland boy!"

"So am I, Harry," I said with more than a little pride.

During my visit I had been checking my wristwatch every few minutes to see how far behind schedule I was for the day. I had already met with my big client, Classic Chevrolet, that morning and I figured I could take no more than an hour between sales calls to finally stop by Mayview and visit my old friend.

But now I was feeling embarrassed that my priorities were so screwed up. I took off my watch and stuffed it into my pocket.

"You want to take a walk outside?" Harry asked, once again turning his attention to the grounds beneath his window.

"Are you allowed off the ward?" I was surprised.

"Sure," he said, "I just have to sign out."

Inadvertently, I looked down at my wrist where my watch had been. "I have all the time in the world," I stated emphatically. And I resolved not to think about my job for the rest of the day.

"Let me get cleaned up first." Harry sounded excited as he went into the bathroom and closed the door. I was a little shocked when I heard the shower come on. I settled back into the fake leather chair and waited.

"I guess I should be honored," I whispered to myself.

Ten minutes later we were in the lobby, signing the grounds pass the gargoyle nurse had provided us. She looked surprised at Harry's clean face and shampooed hair. "Well, don't you look nice," she said haltingly. The crud around his lips was gone; so was the mucous in the corners of his eyes. He was wearing white socks and clean blue jeans with a Notre Dame sweatshirt. There was energy in his step and, even with his toothless grin, he looked ten years younger than when I first saw him.

Soon we were out walking the tree-covered grounds surrounding the institution. "So we played ball all summer," Harry began. "What else did we do?"

"What do you remember?" I said, wondering where the holes in his past started and how big they had become.

Harry lowered his head.

"You said you knew Stephanie, Connie, and Linda. What do you remember about them?" I asked.

"Just the names," he responded.

"And Sammy and the Dillon boys?" I continued.

"Were they my friends, too?" He was still looking down at his feet. "Like you and Tony?"

"Well, they were your friends," I told him, "but not like me and Tony." I thought my words would cheer him up, but he just kept looking at the ground.

"You don't really know who they were, do you?" I asked him earnestly. Then I paused for about a minute. "Harry," I said finally, "do you remember who *you* were?"

"I was a baseball player," he said after some hesitation, "but I can't think of anything else. I mean, what else did we do?"

"We played!" I said, slapping him on the back. "We played all day every day. We rode bikes and went swimming and caught frogs and grasshoppers. We flipped baseball cards. And in the evenings we played Release."

"Release," Harry said, beaming. "I loved Release!"

"Me too," I laughed.

Could they be wrong about his condition? I wondered. *Sure, there are huge holes in his memory, he's toothless and unkempt, but basically, it's the same guy.*

I pushed ahead.

chapter ten

The Lure of Release

Our neighborhood was perfect for a game of Release. The boundaries were Fourth Avenue and Sixth Avenue. With no fences or hedges dividing the lawns, it was like one big yard, about a million square feet of houses, trees, bushes, and sheds; the perfect mix of light and shadow.

The game itself was a cross between hide-and-seek and kick-the-can. It wasn't just an athletic competition, it was a social event. It was an outdoor party, and kids from all over Rockland would come to the neighborhood to be a part of it.

During the baseball game with Steve's Barbershop, Sammy had been circulating through the stands, organizing a group of about twenty kids to play. The Release game was set for 8:15, and those of us who had just finished playing baseball stayed in uniform to save time.

For some reason, Tony insisted on going home first. We figured it was because he was afraid to get grass stains on his baseball pants. Our mothers always warned us not to ruin our uniforms, but usually nobody listened. "I'll be there in ten minutes," Tony shouted as he hopped on his bike after the game and headed home.

I knew he'd be there on time. His girlfriend was playing and so was mine. Pam and Molly were among the group of kids who had to be home before the streetlights came on at about nine o'clock. The rest of us had a curfew of ten o'clock. In fact, at exactly 10 p.m. a fire siren would howl that could be heard all over Rockland. It meant that no one under the age of eighteen was allowed on the streets. It was the official town curfew, but of course, this was Rockland; if the police patrolmen recognized you, they just told you to go home.

In order to save time, Harry and I picked up teams so that we could start right at 8:15. We flipped a coin and Harry won the first pick. He took Tony. I got the next two and took Nelson and Sammy. Nelson was an average baseball player but a great Release player. He was fast and quick and he could climb a tree in seconds. This was useful both for hiding and for capturing tree-climbers from the opposing team.

Harry picked Billy Conti, an eleven-year-old from the other side of town. At this point, I picked Molly. She was a lousy Release player, but she was my girlfriend and I'd rather be hiding with her behind a bush somewhere than have her out there roaming around with somebody else.

Just as we finished picking our teams, Tony came rolling up on his bike. "What the hell are you supposed to be?" gasped Sammy, as we all turned to take in the show. Tony was wearing black Converse, black jeans and a black long-sleeved turtleneck jersey. He looked like a cat burglar.

"It's my Illya shirt," he said smugly. Illya was a character on one of the coolest shows on TV, *The Man from U.N.C.L.E.* It was a secret-agent show that aired weekly during the height of the popularity of the James Bond movies. It starred Robert Vaughn as Napoleon Solo and David McCallum as his partner, Illya Kuryakin. Whenever they were on a mission, Illya always wore a black turtleneck. We all loved the show, but we didn't quite know what to make of Tony in this strange get-up.

If it had been anyone else, we would have poked fun at him all night, but Tony was always a step ahead of us when it came to new fads like Duncan yo-yos and Aurora race cars. Plus, the dark outfit *was* functional for playing Release, a game of stealth and shadows. So no one said anything else derogatory.

The teams weren't exactly even. Harry and Tony were the oldest, but since Tony was late, I had to be a team captain. That put them both on the same team along with Billie, another athletic eleven-year-old. Then when I picked Molly for reasons other than her skill level, it left us a little outclassed. "We hide first," I called out, even though the tradition was to flip a coin for who went first.

Harry looked over his troops. "Go ahead," he said with an air of superiority. And we all ran in different directions looking for a place to hide as Harry and his team counted to fifty.

The rules of the game were pretty simple. Our team would hide and their team would try to find us. Whenever a member of the hiding team was caught, that person would be brought back to base, where he or she would remain a prisoner, surrounded by guards from the capturing team. It was called "Release" because if another member of the hiding team could get past the guards and touch the base, all his teammates would be freed to hide again.

For that reason, the more prisoners that were taken, the more guards that were posted around them. I'm sure the game had its roots in the military, and other team games like kick-the-can couldn't compare for sheer excitement and action. We loved this game!

Plus, it had the added elements of romance and heroism. Where else could you hide out with a pretty girl or *capture* one? Where else could you be a hero, rescuing your teammates from their jailers?

Base for this evening was the telephone pole on Fifth Avenue, across the street from Connie's house. It was under a street lamp so that the game could continue after dark.

Molly and I ran a long way toward my house and hid behind a lilac bush next to my porch. The conversation came easy. It always did with her. We talked about the baseball game and my "home run." We talked about going swimming with a group of friends on Saturday. We talked about how much time we had left until the street lights came on.

We were only ten years old, so our actual contact was pretty limited. Sometimes we would hold hands while we were skating during a couples skate at the local roller rink. Sometimes we would slow dance at a party. But mostly, I just called her my girlfriend and she called me her boyfriend and we didn't care who knew it.

After fifteen minutes or so, I could hear commotion coming from the base area. So we moved closer to get a better look. Six of our eight teammates had already been captured. Bo, Stephanie, Harry, and his little brother Kenny were guarding the base.

We quickly put together an attack strategy. Molly would sacrifice herself by running toward the base and then slant off toward Bellissimos' house. I would wait until one, or hopefully two, of the guards chased her, then I would sweep in and weave my way past the remaining guards to touch the base and free our troops.

A mere *tag* didn't constitute a capture. The guard would have to have a firm grip on me for a bona-fide *catch*. Once I released our teammates, I'd come back to release Molly as soon as I had an opportunity.

The plan didn't work. Only little Kenny chased the decoy. So when I made my move, Harry and Bo were able to trap me before I could reach the base. We both ended up being captured. Now only two of our guys were still in hiding.

Eight of us were already caught, but we huddled around the telephone pole, talking strategy. There was a second way to release our team. The rules stated that as long as we maintained contact with the pole and one another, we could *pull* one of the guards into the base. Once he made contact with the pole, we were free. Of course, the bigger the guard, the harder it was to drag him to the base.

All eight of us now held hands, with the innermost teammate, Lonnie, wrapping his arm around the telephone pole. We stretched out like a giant python, trying to snag the nearest guard. But they were all careful to keep their distance as they watched out for our next attacker. Only Linda and Nelson were still in hiding, and Harry called for more guards to shore up their defenses.

He now posted six guards, with their remaining four soldiers roaming the neighborhood hunting for Nelson and Linda. Within five minutes, I noticed a rustling noise coming from behind a row of pine trees about thirty yards from the base.

"Get ready," I whispered, as the human chain of arms and bodies coiled and uncoiled in the direction of the closest enemy guard. Linda was the first to appear, making a mad dash toward the base and then away again, cutting back into Connie's yard. Then Nelson made his move. It was the same plan of attack Molly and I had used and looked just as futile. Two guards chased Linda while Nelson zigged and zagged wildly trying to avoid capture.

Harry was screaming at the top of his lungs for reinforcements as Nelson weaved in and out between the guards. But, with all the attention and excitement focused on Nelson's attack, little Kenny wandered over behind Harry and Bo to form a second line of defense.

"Don't get too close!" Tony shouted as Kenny kept backing up. Too late! The human chain, with Lonnie at the base and Sammy at the end, coiled around the seven-year-old and dragged him toward the telephone pole. "Release!" we all shouted as Kenny made contact with the base.

We scattered in all directions as three of the enemy soldiers wrestled Nelson to the ground. In the ensuing melee four of my teammates were recaptured, while the rest of us scrambled to freedom.

It took another twenty minutes for them to finally take our entire team into custody; not bad for such a weak army. Now it was their turn to hide. But it was getting dark and Pam, Molly, and a couple other kids from across town said their goodbyes and headed home to beat the streetlights.

It was now an eight-on-eight game. They were bigger and quicker than us. So after half an hour we had captured only five of their soldiers. As captain and biggest member of our team, I stayed with the guards to avoid any loss of prisoners, while Sammy, Lonnie, and Nelson did most of the hunting out in the neighborhood.

Finally only Tony remained at large. It was getting near curfew time and in my frustration I decided to take a calculated risk and send our four best players out to find him. Lonnie and I swept around the right side of Connie's house, while Nelson and Sammy searched the left side.

My plan backfired almost immediately. Tony was hiding in the shadow of Connie's porch, and Lonnie and I walked right past him without noticing. He saw his opportunity and made a break for the base. Three of our four guards were out of position and by the time I saw Tony attacking, he was just fifteen yards from the telephone pole with only Connie in place to stop him.

"Here comes Tony!" I shouted in futility. He was quick and strong and no ten-year-old girl was going to be able to grasp and hold him firmly enough for an official capture. But Connie was determined. As Tony made a quick cut to the left, she grabbed the cuff of his long-sleeved jersey and held on like a pit bull.

Riiippp! I could hear the sound from twenty yards away. Tony stopped dead in his tracks. "My Illya shirt!" he screamed in anguish.

"Oh my God!" cried Connie. "I'm so sorry." As alarming as it seemed at the time, I kept my head in the game and ran up, grabbing Tony by the shoulders.

"Get your hands off me," he shouted, pushing me away from him.

"As long as you know you're captured," I stated matter-of-factly.

Connie, still holding the long black sleeve in her hand, burst into tears, while Tony, whose right arm was now bare up to his shoulder, kept shouting in rage, "You're going to pay for this shirt. You're going to pay!"

Then it started. First a giggle from Nelson, then a chuckle from Sammy, and finally Harry started singing the "Secret Agent Man" theme song. *There's a man who leads a life of danger. To everyone he meets he stays a stranger.* I joined in and so did Linda, then so did everyone else, louder and louder. Now everyone was laughing hysterically. Even Tony cracked a smile as we sang out the final lines, *Secret Agent Man… Secret Agent Man, they've given you a number and taken away your name.*

It was getting late, but no one wanted to leave. We all just sat in the grass, giving the instant replay of "the Illya Affair" from ten or twelve different vantage points. Every time someone retold the story we all laughed wildly again. Finally we heard the fire siren howling and we all sprinted for our houses. It was the official town curfew and our parents would be waiting.

Nelson went straight to bed as soon as we got in the house. I had a late-night bowl of Cheerios while watching TV with my mom and dad, and then I too headed up the stairs. "Brush your teeth," my mother called, "I'll be up in a minute to tuck you in."

"Don't forget to say your prayers," my father added. "And, Ted, nice hit tonight."

I fell asleep as soon as my head hit the pillow. My last thought was, "That was a pretty good day." I was living in paradise and didn't even know it.

chapter eleven

El Productos

Sitting on a cement bench under some oak trees on the hospital campus, Harry couldn't contain his excitement. "The Illya shirt," he laughed, "I remember that. I really *do* remember that… and Tony's bare arm… and Connie was crying." And we both cracked up again.

Then just as he did in 1964, Harry's eyes filled with tears as he tried to contain his snickering. *Wow,* I thought, *this isn't just a five-year-old listening to a funny story. This is a genuine memory.*

"Hey, let's go to the commissary," Harry said suddenly, his flight of ideas still very much a distraction.

"Where is it?" I asked. And Harry led the way.

We walked into the commissary through an outside door at ground level. "Do you have any money?" he whispered as we approached two women in white skirts and blouses behind the counter. "Sure," I nodded, "get whatever you want."

The counter looked like a newsstand, with packs of gum and magazines and candy bars, but it also was wide enough to have a grill built into the wall behind it. The smell of hamburgers and deep-fried mushrooms filled the air.

"Hi, Harry," one of the counter girls said brightly, her eyes diverting so as not to engage him in any real conversation. "What can I get for you?"

Harry looked at his feet for a second. "Can I get some cigars?" he asked me finally.

"Do they allow smoking on the ward?" I wondered out loud.

"Everybody up there smokes," Harry reassured me, and the counter lady nodded her agreement.

"Cigars it is then," I told her. And she looked to Harry for the brand. "Give me a box of El Productos," he beamed.

A box… I thought he would grab a cigar or two; maybe a little pocket-sized pack of stogies; but a box? That's twenty-four cigars! The woman in white looked at me in astonishment and waited for a signal that it was okay to fill his order.

Harry was grinning from ear to ear. He knew he sucked me into this. He heard me say "get whatever you want," and now he was going to pull my chain... unbelievable!

"Get him the cigars," I told the lady. "You know, Harry," I deadpanned, "you're still an asshole."

"That's right, I *am*," Harry shot back. He seemed delighted to be something other than pathetic and brain-damaged and mentally ill.

"I'm an asshole." And we both couldn't stop laughing.

I had about fifty dollars on me and the cigars cost thirty-two. "You said you remembered the woods," I said as I handed the box over to Harry and we made our way back to the courtyard. "Do you remember the trestle?"

"The trestle." Harry's eyes lit up. "Where Sammy yelled, 'minnies' and Tony stepped on the nail?"

"That's right," I said, marveling at the chips and pieces of childhood memories he still had stored away.

"And where Carlo caught all those frogs in one day?"

"That's the greatest trestle story of all!" I grinned. "But, Harry," I looked him in the eye now. "Do you remember what happened to those frogs?" He began to look distressed again.

"Come on, Harry," I coached. "What makes this the greatest trestle story of all time?"

chapter twelve

Frogs, Minnows, and Crayfish

"Hey, Teddeee." The choir was back outside my window the next morning. "Hey, Teddeee." I looked down from my bedroom. It was quite a group: Sammy, Harry, Tony, Bo, Lonnie, and Sammy's little cousin Carlo. There was one difference: no baseball gloves. Instead they carried fishing nets, and Bo had a five-gallon bait can.

"What's up?" I shouted down to them. "We're going to the trestle," Sammy replied. "Hurry up!"

Nelson was up and out of bed before I could even turn around. He loved going to the trestle, which was the arched cement bridge that carried the railroad tracks over a small stream in the woods. Of course it was the creek that was the attraction, but we never said we were going to the creek. We always said we were going to the trestle.

The tracks ran parallel to Fourth Avenue, just fifteen yards in front of my house, and the nameless stream was just a half-mile down the tracks. It was teaming with frogs and minnows and crayfish, which look like miniature lobsters. We also caught a few tadpoles, lizards, and the occasional turtle.

The stream ran for miles from the west and all the way east to the Beaver River. At its widest it was about twenty feet across, but averaged about five feet. It had a series of pools and small waterfalls and was never more than two feet deep.

Within minutes, eight of us were walking down the railroad tracks south into the woods. There was a ditch that ran alongside the tracks, and along the way we stopped and pulled out a couple rusty, discarded paint cans. We would use these to carry back minnows and crayfish. Any frogs we caught would go into the bait can that Bo was carrying. Minnows and crayfish couldn't escape, but frogs could and would jump out of any container that didn't have a lid. Even when we were adding a new catch to the can, we had to be careful not to allow any of the prisoners to escape.

"Me and Lonnie came down here last week," Bo offered. "We saw about ten frogs upstream and tons of minnows just below the falls downstream." The nets we carried were homemade from broomsticks and wire hangers. And the netting itself had very tiny holes too small for minnows to slip through. Harry's mother, who made extra money as a freelance seamstress, had given us the netting material and showed us how to sew it to the rounded hangers.

Before we had the nets, we caught minnows in small jars and would bring home about two or three per trip. With the nets, we averaged fifteen to twenty each day. We now caught enough to *sell* them to the rest of the neighborhood kids. Minnows and crayfish were priced at a penny a piece, frogs were a nickel, and a nice turtle could sell for 50 cents! We kept them all in a big tub under my porch. At times it looked like a small aquarium. At the height of our season, we probably made about a dollar a week, which we would split six ways.

Because of the rocky stream bed, frogs and crayfish still had to be caught by hand. We had three nets with us that day. The remaining five of us would be on frog and crayfish duty.

It took about ten minutes to reach the stream from my house, unless a train came by us. Then, the first one to see it would scream, "Train!" and we would scramble off the tracks and stand along the railroad bed until it passed. Most of the trains were carrying freight back and forth between the different departments of the steel mill. Every once in a while a passenger train would pass, and the people on board would always smile and wave at us.

With our fishing nets and cans, we must have looked like a small band of Indians out on a hunt. I can still remember the envious looks in those passengers' eyes, especially the men in suits with briefcases in their laps and sad smiles on their faces. Or maybe I don't remember; I just think I do.

When we reached the stream, we had to scale down the side of the hill from the railroad bed to the water. The trestle was built into the hillside and dropped down diagonally to the stream in giant six-foot concrete steps. It was a little dangerous, but we were all experts at scaling the concrete slabs and climbed down to the stream in minutes.

"Let's check out the minnows first," Tony suggested, as we all headed downstream. The surrounding trees and vines kept most of the stream in constant shade, but dapples of sunlight flickered here and there across the water.

We walked along the pathway beside the stream until we reached a small waterfall that opened up into a pool about a foot deep and fifteen feet across. The minnows were out swimming in the sunny side of the pool and we had to approach slowly and quietly. Any quick move or shadow we cast on the water would spook the small fish and they would disappear into the rocks and tiny underwater caves along the edges of the stream.

"There they are," Harry whispered, taking charge of the mission. "Nelson, circle around between them and the rocks." Nelson took one of the nets and crept slowly over to the bottom of the three-foot waterfalls, cutting off the minnows' escape route to their homes.

The key to catching minnows was to get it right the first time. If someone spoke too loudly or splashed the water or moved too quickly, the little fish would be gone in an instant and wouldn't come back out into the pool for about twenty minutes. Harry and Sammy took the other two nets and moved slowly on either side along the tree line beside the water, trying to keep their shadows from falling across the stream.

They crawled out toward the water like a cat approaching a chipmunk until they were only three feet from the water's edge.

The school of minnows was still basking in the sunlit pool. "Now!" Harry ordered, as he and Sammy lunged forward, sweeping their nets into the water. The minnows streaked away in all directions, but most headed toward the rocks at the foot of the falls, where Nelson was waiting. He timed his net perfectly, scooping it directly into the school of terrified fish.

"I got three," Harry laughed triumphantly as he examined the contents of his net. "I got two," Sammy added.

Nelson looked down into his net and said nothing, but his face lit up like a five-year-old's on Christmas morning. "I don't know," he stammered. "I can't count them all!" We broke into a cheer of joy, hugs, and congratulations.

"At least a dozen," Nelson bragged, "and two of them are monsters." Normal fish in this little stream were about an inch-and-a-half long. The biggest one in

Nelson's net was about twice that length. When the counting was done, we had twenty-one "minnies."

We filled one of the old paint cans about half full and plopped the fish into the water. We added a few pebbles and some water plants to make them feel at home.

We were still bubbling with excitement as we made our way further downstream. At one point, the right side of the shore became too steep and we had to cross over to the left-side path. We could have made our way across the water by slowly hopping from one rock to the next, but Mother Nature provided a much more entertaining means of transportation. There were hundreds of wild grape vines hanging from the tree tops. I grabbed one and pulled down on it as hard as I could. It broke free from a few of the weaker branches, then held fast to the stronger ones. As soon as I was sure it would support my full weight, I took a few steps back, then ran forward, swinging across the stream and landing cleanly on the other side.

I then tossed the vine back to the rest of the tribe and one by one my buddies rode the vine across the water. We were like eight little Tarzans, and howled the Tarzan call as we swung through the air.

We didn't have much success with minnows farther down the stream. We were making too much noise and the fish got spooked before we could get close enough to net them. We turned over some rocks and caught three or four crayfish.

The trick to catching crayfish was to anticipate which way they would swim after we flipped the rocks. Crayfish would always propel themselves backward underwater by flexing their tails underneath them.

If they were cornered, the small lobster-like crustaceans would raise their claws and open them as wide as possible, snapping at our fingers and hands. I learned quickly that the only way to catch one without getting pinched by its claws was to grab it by the midsection, just behind the head. If you grabbed the tail, it could flip out of your grip. If you grabbed the claws, it would snap at your fingers. Getting pinched by a crayfish wasn't terribly painful and almost never drew blood, but it was scary and the claws on the little bastards were intimidating.

We went downstream about a hundred yards and caught five crayfish. I caught three of them. The last one was a new mother. I have no idea how crayfish procreate, but this one had ten tiny babies clinging to the bottom of her tail. "Put it back," Tony suggested, when we noticed the babies. I hesitated. "Look how tiny they are," I marveled. "I want my mom to see them."

"They'll die," Tony replied. I knew he was right. I should put this brood back into the water. That's what the nuns at St. Teresa's School would have told us to do.

"That's the coolest thing I've ever seen," Harry chimed in. "Keep them if you want them." Everyone but Tony nodded in agreement and I put the whole litter into the paint can. I still regret it to this day.

"Let's get some frogs," Tony shrugged, changing the subject. We headed back upstream, swinging on vines and chattering as we went. We finally passed back under the trestle and into the marshy part of the stream where the frogs were breeding.

The very best area for catching frogs was the place where the stream divided in two and then flowed back together again. That left a small, wet, grassy "island" between the forks. It was frog heaven.

The problem with the island was that it was almost impossible to keep your feet dry. In the lower part of the stream there were lots of rocks and vines and a solid bank, but here, one wrong step could sink your shoe into a foot of mud. Most of us wore old shoes when we went to the trestle, but today Sammy was sporting a brand-new pair of sneakers and was determined to keep them clean.

One by one each of us took a misstep and soaked at least one sneaker. By the time we reached the island, only Sammy still had two dry feet. Although we were moving upstream as quietly as possible, the frogs sensed we were coming and we could hear them jump from the banks into the water as we approached.

"Let the water settle," Nelson suggested, as we all took our places along the edge of the stream. Finally I could make out the image of a frog half-buried by the mud he'd squirmed into.

Since my sneakers were already wet, I waded into the water until I was standing right over the frog-shaped lump in the mud. In one quick motion, I thrust my hand into the silt and pulled up a beauty—big and long and bright green. Tony named him "Green Bay" almost immediately, and I carefully placed him into the trap door of Bo's five-gallon bait can.

We had it about one-third full of water, and Green Bay plopped into the can and immediately began leaping and hopping and struggling to get out. A few minutes later, Lonnie pulled a nice-sized brown-and-yellow specimen out of the reeds. Then Tony grabbed a little all-brown frog off the bank. This frog had big, bright yellow eyes and I dubbed him "Cat's Eyes" as Tony carefully dropped him into the bait can, making sure that none of the captives jumped out while the new prisoner was being incarcerated.

Within an hour, we had six frogs, and only little Carlo Bellissimo, Sammy's cousin, had failed to contribute to the day's catch. Suddenly, Carlo screamed, "I got one!" as cheers went up from the whole hunting party. He beamed as we congratulated him, one after another.

Two minutes later, Carlo had another frog, and five minutes after that a third one. He was on fire! Carlo was hunting in the highest reeds in the marshiest part of the stream and a couple of us went into the same area, guessing that he must have discovered a virtual *nest* of frogs. Carlo was only seven years old, but I had never seen anyone catch frogs at the rate he was pulling them out of the water.

Incredibly, it happened again. "I got another one!" Carlo screamed. This one was a beauty, big and bright green, a dead ringer for Green Bay. But as Carlo tried to slide him into the bait can, the big fellow slithered between his fingers and leaped to freedom, out into the middle of the widest part of the stream.

We were all determined to get him back and scoured the area looking for any trace of him in the mud. Finally I spotted the outline of a big frog in the silt on the opposite shoreline. Sammy attempted to cross the stream by hopping from rock to rock, but the last stone was particularly slimy and his brand-new sneakers were brand-new no more. "Damn it," he cried out as he pulled his mud-covered shoe from the bottom of the creek, "this is war!"

Now Nelson and I closed in from the island side of the stream. It took another ten minutes, but I finally grabbed the green monster and took him to the bait can to make sure he didn't slip away again. I stuffed him under the lid, and then took a quick look inside to admire our day's catch. Yep, there they were, six pairs of slimy eyes poking out of the water.

"Six?" I screamed. "There should be ten frogs here! How'd we lose four frogs?"

"What are you talking about?" Bo yelled. "Where did they go?"

It was Sammy who first saw the light. "You son of a bitch!" he screamed at Carlo. "You never caught one damn frog. All you did was grab *our* frogs and shake them around in the water."

We were all angry, but Sammy was livid. He stood there in his mud-covered, formerly white sneakers. "Get his feet," he barked at Bo, as he grabbed Carlo under his armpits. We all counted out loud as they swung him back and forth, "One… two… three!" And they let him fly. Out into the deepest part of the stream he flew, under the water and then back up again, gagging and gasping for air. Slowly he got to his feet, soaked from head to toe.

For a second I thought he was going to cry, but I didn't care. I was still furious. Not only did we have six frogs instead of ten, but we just wasted twenty minutes recapturing our prized catch of the day. Then Carlo did something amazing. He burst into laughter. He was covered in mud and he was laughing. His mother was going to kill him, and he kept on laughing. His friends all hated him, and the tears in his eyes were tears of happiness.

We went to the trestle maybe thirty times each summer for maybe seven years. We caught hundreds of frogs and crayfish, thousands of minnows. I carried a million "trestle stories" with me the rest of my life, but the one I remember the most, the one that always makes me smile, is Carlo's hot streak.

It only took a minute for us all to see the humor. For a very short time, Carlo wasn't a seven-year-old; he was our hero. He wasn't extra baggage; he was the main man. Of course, we razzed him mercilessly for years, but I guess he thought it was worth it, the little bastard.

chapter thirteen

The Lucky Ones

"That's right," shouted Harry, leaping up from the courtyard bench. "That's right. The little bastard didn't catch any frogs. He didn't catch any frogs at all!"

It was early October, and about half a dozen squirrels had been busy gathering acorns from the grounds around the hospital. But Harry's booming voice sent them scattering in unison across the shady courtyard and up the trunks of the oak trees that towered over us.

"Take it easy, Harry," I chuckled, "you're scaring the forest creatures."

He was beaming from ear to ear like the toothless old man with his fishing pole in that painting by Norman Rockwell. The change in Harry was undeniable. Gone were the pale face and tired eyes that had greeted me on the ward. His cheeks were rosy from the cool autumn air and his eyes sparkled with life.

"You got a light?" He laughed as he unwrapped one of his El Productos.

"I think there's a pack of matches in the bag," I told him.

He touched a match to the cigar and puffed mightily six or seven times until the tip glowed. "You got an extra one of those?" I said expectantly.

"Get your own," he deadpanned. It was vintage Harry humor.

"What an asshole," I barked, as I grabbed a cigar from his lap and lit it up. And we both sat back on the bench, chuckling and shaking our heads in mock displeasure.

Ten minutes passed and no one said a word. I could tell my visit had started the rusty gears of memory turning in Harry's mind and I wondered where they would lead us. The squirrels had crawled back down the trees and were once again foraging around the grounds as a light breeze sent waves of sunshine and shadow dancing across the lawn. Harry took one deep drag on his El Producto and let out a long sigh. I knew the conversation was about to take a darker turn.

"Teddy," he whispered, "why did this happen to me?"

Shit, I thought. *I'm not ready for this.* I recalled my phone conversation with Janie Kirkland the day before. "He's like a child, Teddy," she had told me. "Don't be upset if he doesn't remember you at all." Her comments had been unsettling, but deep down I had been a little relieved that I wouldn't have to face this question, the unanswerable question.

"I don't know, Harry," I said finally. "I don't know why these things happen to anyone." I knew my answer was weak and hollow and hopeless, but I didn't know what else to say.

"Why didn't I just die?" he continued. "Why didn't God just take me? Why did He leave me like this?" And we both lowered our heads and sat in silence.

Now the sunshine and the shadows and the trees and the bright October afternoon seemed to close in around us, and the scent of the approaching winter sent a cold chill down my back.

"Our fathers," Harry was choking back tears now, "they were the lucky ones."

I felt a spontaneous wave of anger surge through my veins. What was this brain-damaged, five-year-old son of a bitch saying? When I was seventeen, my father had died unexpectedly of a heart attack at age forty-five. He was never sick a day in his life. Everyone at the funeral kept saying, "At least he didn't suffer" as if that made it better; as if that mattered to a kid whose life had just been shattered. "He's *lucky* he went so quickly and now he's with God." Every time they opened their mouths it made me furious. But I had to just stand there and shake their hands and nod my head and pretend I was a man.

Two weeks before my father's heart attack, Harry's father had passed away shockingly of a stroke at age fifty. Two doors apart; two sudden deaths; two grieving families; what's so "lucky" about that?

"What's that mean?" I shot back, hardly concealing my disgust as my old frustration crashed to the surface. "What the hell are you talking about?"

"I know they died." Harry covered his face in shame. "But they were like heroes. Everyone was sad. The whole town came to the funeral home and everyone cried. Who cried for me, Teddy? Who even knows I'm alive? I just wish it would have ended then, and people would have said 'poor Harry,' and they would have told funny stories about me, and they would have missed me, and they would have still… still…"

"Cared about you?" My voice was calmer now.

"Do you know how many of my friends have visited me?" Harry was barely audible. "I mean besides my family?" I shook my head.

"You're the first one." He was sobbing now and I felt ashamed of my anger and lack of compassion. It surprised me that he didn't even remember Tony's visit. But I realized that callers in this place were a rare occurrence.

Harry had been at Mayview for nearly fifteen years. And while I had lived in Boston with my family for most of that time, I had been back in Western Pennsylvania for eighteen months and just never got around to visiting my old childhood friend. "He won't forget today," I vowed under my breath. "I won't let him forget."

"Do they remember me, Teddy?" He was speaking in a whisper. "Does anyone ever mention me?"

I put my hand on his shoulder. It was boney and frail with no hint of the athletic arm that could once throw out a runner from deep in the hole behind third base. "*I* remember, Harry. I remember it all. And so do Tony and Sammy and Jiggy."

"What about the rest of Rockland? Do they remember who I am; who I was?"

I grabbed Harry by both shoulders now but he turned away, so I shook him until he looked me straight in the eyes.

"Who gives a shit what they remember? Who cares what they think?" I was shouting now and the squirrels flew back up the trees in terror. "No wonder you're so depressed and angry. No wonder you look like you're eighty years old. You have no idea who you are! Hell, one good breeze could blow you away, and you wouldn't even care."

"Who am I, Teddy? I mean, who was I?"

"I don't want to hear that shit anymore either, Harry. Who you were *is* who you are. Don't you think *I'm* the same kid who caught frogs and chased girls and made the all-star team when I was ten years old? That *is* who I am. That's who I'll always be. No matter how many bosses get on my back, no matter how many clients slam their doors in my face, I'm still Ted Tresh, goddamn it, and you're still Harry Kirkland!"

"I don't remember, Teddy."

Suddenly I knew why I was there that day. I knew I wasn't going back to work. I knew my wristwatch was no longer a factor. "Let's go back inside," I whispered. "I want you to take another look at the newspaper photo I brought you. I'm going to tell you about our Little League all-star team."

chapter fourteen

The Rockland Little League All-Stars

So it went that summer, day after day... pick-up games or frog hunting in the mornings; chatting up the neighborhood girls in the afternoons; dinner at the kitchen table with my brother, sisters, and parents at exactly 5:15 every day; Little League games until dusk; Release games until curfew. What I wouldn't give to have one of those days back!

But it wasn't all fun and games that summer. Starting on July 1, the routine was about to get a lot more intense. That's the day we waited for all year: the day Johnny Gallo, the coach of the Rockland Little League All-Stars, announced his eighteen-man roster. This team wouldn't just play against teams from our little town; this team would represent Rockland in two big tournaments during July and August. The whole town followed this team.

They would face the best Little League players and the best Little League teams from all over Western Pennsylvania and Eastern Ohio. For the next two months, this team would be the major focus of Rockland, the immigrant town, the steel town still battling for its identity. It was a fight for affirmation and this all-star team was the weapon of choice.

If you were named to the all-star team, you became a minor celebrity in Rockland. If you didn't make it, you felt like a second-class ballplayer, just another body used to fill out the rosters of Rockland's four-team league.

Any boy who was eight to twelve years old and had a pulse could play in the Rockland Little League. But to be an all-star you had to be able to hit and field and bunt and run the bases. You had to know the game almost as well as the adults, and you had to be willing to work your ass off. Coach Gallo was a teacher at a nearby high school. He had the summers off and had plenty of time to whip the team into shape. Plus, he was a cousin to Uncle Joe, and like everyone else in our extended family, he lived and died baseball. The Rockland Little League All-Stars practiced twice a day, from 10 a.m. to noon and from one to three every afternoon.

The town was always obsessed with this team, but even more so this year. John Kennedy was just eight months in the grave, and it seemed that the world had changed overnight. For the first time since the end of WWII, no one seemed to know who really ran the country. I think our veteran fathers were shaken by the feeling that there might be men in the shadows calling the shots. They had patriotically supported the Korean War, turned a blind eye to McCarthy's tactics, and grudgingly tolerated the government's Cold War policies. But the assassination was even more ominous. There was an uneasy feeling everywhere.

But the spring of '64 followed the winter of '63. And when baseball season returned, so did the attention of the town. They were looking for something familiar, something close to their hearts; something to believe in. And in 1964, more than any other year, they decided to put their faith in this baseball team.

They had good reason to be optimistic. Most people in town thought that this might be the best Little League team to come out of Rockland in the last twenty years. Not only had the 1963 team won a few games in the big New Castle Tournament, but the team had actually won the *championship* of the suburban New Galilee Tournament. And six starters from that team would be back for the 1964 team, including one of the best pitching prospects in the state, Derrick Dawson.

The New Galilee Tournament did not allow teams from the cities to compete; no Ellwood City, no Beaver Falls, no New Castle, no New Brighton. But it was still very competitive, with the best township and small-town teams from a four-county area, teams like Bessemer, Shenango, Highland, Big Beaver and Darlington Township. These were towns with populations four or five times that of Rockland's 900 residents. It was a tremendous accomplishment for the '63 team to win that tournament, and the '64 team was expected to be even better.

My Board of Trade team had a six-o'clock game on July 1, and everyone knew that immediately after the game, the all-star roster would be posted on the wall of the concession stand. I could still remember my disappointment in '63, when, as a nine-year-old, I didn't make the team. In fact, no eight- or nine-year-olds in the league had been named to the all-stars that year, but that didn't soothe my wounded ego. Harry and Tony had both made the '63 team and I knew I could compete with either of them.

I remember going into my uncle Joe's drugstore on the first day of all-star practice in '63 to drown my sorrow with a cherry coke. "Why aren't you at all-star practice?" my uncle had chastised me.

"I didn't make the team!" I barked back at him.

"I don't give a shit if you made the team or not. Get down there and learn something." I wasn't sure my nine-year-old ego was ready for that, but I decided to swallow my pride, take Uncle Joe's advice, and just show up for every practice anyway.

Turns out, the coaches were always looking for some extra players to "catch in" while they hit fly balls to the outfielders, to run the bases for bunting and base-stealing workouts, and to play in intra-squad games. I just kept coming to practice day after day at 10 a.m. and 1 p.m. Eventually, I got up the nerve to go out and take infield practice with the rest of the all-star infielders. I figured if the coach wanted me off the field, he would tell me to get off the field—but he never did.

I made a point of diving for every ground ball in the hole and smothering every bad hop by letting it bounce off my chest or arms or legs. I ignored the teasing from the older players who thought I was getting in their way or slowing down their practice time. I also ignored the other nine-year-olds in town who called me a phony and said I had no right to be there. I just listened and learned from the coaches and practiced as hard as I could. By July 15, they added my name to the all-star roster.

Of course, I didn't get much playing time. But I did earn my first trophy when we won the 1963 New Galilee Tournament. I was even on the field for the final out when we swamped the Galilee team to win the championship and celebrated by jumping on Dawson's back when he struck out the final batter.

So now I was ten, and I had every reason to believe that my name would be listed among those eighteen players' names posted on that piece of paper hanging from the concession stand door. I knew Johnny Gallo had been scouting every game in May and June and I knew I was having a pretty good season. Still, you could never know for sure.

We had won our game that night, blowing out McDowell's Hotel 10–1. I even had a couple hits, but as I approached the crowd of about thirty kids pushing their way toward the list and peering over each other's shoulders, I could hear them calling out names and mine wasn't among them. I could hear the excitement in the voices of kids who made the team and the anguish of those whose names were not listed. The all-star roster was always controversial, with ballplayers who weren't on the list picking out the weakest names on the list and complaining, "I'm better than he is!" That would be followed by a week of angry calls from angry parents to unapologetic coaches who would patiently defend their choices.

Finally I heard what I was waiting for: twelve-year-old Tommy Rizzo, the third-baseman on my Board of Trade team, unleashing an expletive-laced tirade that ended with the words "I'm better than Teddy Tresh is!" Tony was standing behind me. He didn't need to see the roster. He had started at first base in '63 and was a certain starter again this year. "What's Tommy bitching about?" he asked me.

"Who cares?" I whispered back to him.

"Well, what did he say?" Tony asked again. He wanted an explanation for the outburst.

"He said I made the all-star team," I deadpanned. Among all the other wonders of that great summer, I was beginning to develop the sense of humor I would carry with me into adult life.

"Were you worried?" Tony sounded shocked. "You made it last year, didn't you?"

Tony was a great put-down artist. No one was better at razzing his friends. No one could use sarcasm and wit to tear down his buddies the way Tony could. He hung a horrible nickname on Harry one year that stuck with him until he was fifteen years old. But Tony never put me down. He never razzed me. He never said a bad word about me as far as I know. He was one of the best ballplayers in town, but he always said *we* were the best, that *we* couldn't be beat, that *we* outclassed everyone else. His humor was cutting and sharp and some people really resented him for it. But he was probably the person most responsible for building my self-esteem. I guess that's what best friends do.

"Nah, I wasn't worried," I lied, "I'm going to start this year!"

"I know you will," he replied. But his eyebrows betrayed him, rising inadvertently before he could control them, and I knew he had his doubts. I was a second-baseman, and there were at least four guys on the team who would try out for second base.

"It starts tomorrow at 10 a.m.," I said under my breath, "No ground ball's going to get past me." Then I sighed out loud, "I wish I was hitting better."

"Who's going to beat you out?" Harry now joined the discussion. He had just pitched against McDowell's and was flying high coming off the victory. "I'm going to start at short, Tony at first, and *you* at second. It'll be a Board of Trade infield; the *Red Infield*," Harry sang it out as if we were already famous.

Just then Uncle Joe walked past carrying a canvas bag filled with bats and balls and helmets from the game, heading to his car, where he would stuff them in his trunk.

"Coach," Harry shouted to him, "can you hit us a few ground balls?"

"Now?" replied my uncle. Harry nodded his head.

"Sure, sure," Jiggy beamed. Tony hesitated for a moment, but he didn't dare disappoint his dad.

"All-Star practice starts tomorrow," Harry winked, "and we'll be ready."

So we headed back out onto the ball field, Tony to first, me to second, Harry to short, while all the other ballplayers and fans made their way back home. We fielded grounders, whipped the ball around the bases, turned double plays and chattered repetitive encouragements to one another until it got too dark to see.

Finally we picked up the equipment and helped Uncle Joe carry it to his car. All the while, the molten steel from the Babcock & Wilcox plant beyond the right-field fence crackled and roared and lit up the night sky like fireworks.

chapter fifteen

His Own Little Hell

"I did that?" Harry seemed shocked as we waited at the nurses' station to sign back in to the unit. "I *wanted* to practice?"

"Nobody likes to practice, Harry," I reminded him. "Plus, you and Tony were almost certain to be starters that season."

"Then why would I do that?" He looked positively confused.

"I guess you did it for me, Harry." I playfully smacked him on the back of his head. "You weren't always a selfish bastard."

He wasn't sure if I was praising him or insulting him. There was a time when Harry would have known in an instant that I was really *thanking* him, but his rattled brain cells—combined with years of living on a mental ward— had dulled his awareness. For years he had been living on instinct alone. He lowered his head again. "I don't understand. It doesn't seem like... I mean, I wouldn't..." his voice trailed off.

"It's not your fault, Harry." The words just started gushing out of me. "They brought you here fifteen years ago, right after the attack. You needed to be re-taught everything, but what have you been exposed to since then? Patronizing smiles from the staff and God knows what kind of wild, self-absorbed ramblings from the patients? And I'm not blaming them," I blurted. "They're caught up in their own little worlds—their own little hells."

"Can I help you?" interrupted the pastel nurse who had just arrived at the window of the nurses' station. She had caught the last few lines of the conversation and she wasn't smiling now.

"I need to sign in," Harry stated matter-of-factly, "and I need you to put these in my locker," he continued, handing her the box of cigars.

"Okay, Mr. Kirkland, I'll take care of that." The brightness and merriment were gone from her voice now; she was all business. "Visiting hours will be ending soon," she continued. "You should start saying goodbye to your guest."

"What are you talking about?" Harry shot back. "I'm a voluntary. I can have visitors until eight o'clock. Check my chart."

The nurse's eyes and mouth were both wide open, and she stood there in stunned silence. "C'mon," Harry said, and led the way back to his room.

When we got to 310, a tall black man in hospital pajamas and robe was staring out the window at nothing in particular. "This is my roommate, James," Harry announced loudly. "James, this is my buddy Ted."

The man turned around slowly. He looked about thirty-five and had crooked lower teeth that protruded out beyond his top teeth. He was unshaven and had one long eyebrow across his forehead. "Hey" was all he said.

"James, we need a little privacy." Harry took the big man by the elbow and led him to the door.

"What the hell you talking about, old man?" James moaned as he stumbled across the floor. "Privacy," Harry continued. "Just for a little while." And he ushered James to the hallway and closed the door in his face.

"This is bullshit, Harry," he shouted from the other side. "This is bullshit!" But his voice sounded more amused than angry.

Harry ignored him and headed straight for the framed news clipping on the window sill. "Here." He picked it up and handed it to me. "What does it say?"

"Can't you read?" I asked him calmly.

"I can read. But it gives me a headache. *You* read it. You tell me what was so special about this all-star team."

"I'd be happy to," I responded. "That's the best story of them all—the story of our lives."

Harry sat on his bed and a small smile finally crossed his lips. His self-image was ravaged. His body was frail. His thoughts were chaos and regrets. But somehow he knew something was wrong with this picture. Something didn't fit. A flicker of the old ego was fighting for life.

"I've already told you how good Dawson was," I started slowly, "but I haven't told you how hard we worked. We busted our asses on that ball field. Every day for two months we busted our asses."

Pete had broken his arm earlier that summer and had had the cast removed just forty-eight hours before game time. The arm was still in a sling, which he gingerly removed as he stepped into the batter's box. He looked weak and overmatched, like a wounded soldier, but with two strikes he lined a base hit up the middle, scoring both runners.

The hundred or so Rockland fans in attendance roared their approval. People were jumping up and down, shaking the grandstand. I had never heard or seen such mass happiness in my young life. Pete's mother ran onto the field and hugged her son as she broke down in tears of joy and relief. The little steel town had finally beaten one of the bigger, more-privileged city teams. There wasn't a dry eye in the place.

But the town's joy was short-lived. Because of the broken arm, Pete wasn't expected to play and Coach Gallo had inadvertently left his name off the tournament roster. The next day the tournament officials declared the win invalid and instead awarded the victory to their own Ellwood City team. Rockland was in mourning for months.

This was the legacy we were inheriting: a legacy of tough, hard-working also-rans, a hustling bunch of kids who weren't quite good enough to compete with the city boys. We were the sons and grandsons of immigrants and these older boys were our role models, our heroes, but now Johnny Gallo was saying *we* might be the best he ever had. The responsibility for all those years of frustration was being laid on our shoulders. In that moment, the infighting and jealousies from our own intra-league games seemed unimportant. We were ready to represent our hometown; ready to start playing ball together.

When he finished his pep talk, Coach Gallo sent us out onto the diamond for infield and outfield practice. "Take whatever position you want to play this season," he instructed. "If we need to move you around later, we will."

I ran out to second base, then watched in horror as five other ballplayers ran out and stood beside me. It was worse than I had feared. There were eighteen players on the team and six of them were trying out for second base. I guess the word was out; the best chance of making the starting team was at second. No one but Tony went to first base and no one but Ray Marino went to third. Every other position had only two players trying to fill it. I dug in my cleats, spat in my glove, and waited for the first ground ball.

We took about twenty rounds of infield and outfield practice that morning. I was sweaty and tired and out of breath. I looked more like a hockey goalie than an infielder, and spent most of my time diving for ground balls or knocking them down with my chest or legs or arms. I didn't really catch the ball better than the other guys, but it was obvious that I wouldn't let it get past me. I had a pretty strong arm for a ten-year-old, so when I knocked a ball down I could usually just throw it to first base from my knees.

I could tell the coaches were impressed—and that wasn't easy to accomplish. Besides Johnny Gallo, the coaching staff was made up of some of the best ballplayers ever to come out of Rockland. Johnny's brother Cal and his dad, "Chick" Gallo, who also served as commissioner of the league, came to practice almost every day to help out the infielders. Trippy Blanchard, a twenty-one-year-old Rockland boy who was starting at shortstop for Notre Dame, showed up at least once a week. Younger guys like seventeen-year-old Cam Slater and Timmy Bianchi sacrificed their summers to help out. And, of course, as our chief batting instructor, Uncle Joe would leave the pharmacy for hours at a time, and would only return to the store when my grandfather came down to the field to drag him back to fill prescriptions.

Every time I dove for a ball or took a grounder off my chest, I could hear the coaches shouting their praises for my determination. The morning session ended at noon and by the time we came back at one o'clock for the afternoon practice, two of the six second-basemen had moved to other positions. Dicky Baruby, Beans' brother, had moved over to back up Tony at first base, and Terry Marino had moved to third to back up his brother Ray. My odds of starting were getting better all the time.

The afternoon session was basically for batting practice. Uncle Joe stood right behind the batting cage and loudly instructed each hitter as he took his swings. If you pulled your shoulder away from an outside pitch, he called you a punk; if you took your eye off the ball, he cursed and chided you incessantly. If you stepped away from an inside pitch, he questioned your manhood. There

chapter seventeen

Purgatory

"It must be nice!" Harry looked disgusted as he walked over to his bed and gazed down at the news clipping in front of him.

Despite the look on his face, I thought I detected a hint of humor in Harry's voice. "What must be nice?" I lobbed him the straight line if he wanted it.

"It must be nice to know that you can say you beat me in Elimination and I can't remember if you did or not. Hell, you can tell me anything and I have to believe you."

"You know I'm married to Kim Basinger, right?" I said, tossing him another straight line.

"I'm not that crazy!" he fired back, and we both laughed and smacked each other on the shoulder. It was almost like Harry was back. Maybe this wasn't a waste of time. Maybe I wasn't talking to a ghost after all.

"So you remember Elimination?" I was a little surprised that the game had stuck in his head for so long.

"Catch the ball, you're in. Miss the ball, you're out. Yeah, I remember that," he shot back. "But I don't remember you being better than me."

"That was just the first day," I reminded him. "We played Elimination at the end of every afternoon practice. You brought home your share of broken bats and worn-out baseballs. Lots of different guys won at Elimination, Harry." I put my hand on his shoulder for emphasis. "But you and I were always a *threat* to win. We'd finish in the final five almost every day."

Harry had been smiling during this whole conversation, and I could see his old self-image was starting to return, but now a strange look of bewilderment crossed his face. He looked down at his feet and slowly walked across his hospital room and into his bathroom. He stopped in front of the mirror to check his reflection, as if to verify the doubts that had crept back into his brain. It wasn't a glass mirror at all; it was some type of polished metal. But the metal was slightly warped and scratched, as if someone had been pounding on it.

His reflection was dark and distorted and I stepped in beside him until both our images appeared. The contrast was shocking. He looked so old and thin and toothless and gray.

"I wish I would have died, Teddy." His words were barely audible. "Then people would remember me the way I was. Not like this."

"Sometimes I wake up in the middle of the night and I don't know where I am and I don't know *who* I am, and I think I must be dead. Then they come banging at my door to wake me and I realize it's worse than I thought, worse than being dead. I have to be *this* for another day and the day after that, and the next day." His voice trailed off into nothingness.

"Maybe if I died," he said finally, "maybe I'd be in Heaven. Maybe I'd be happy."

"Maybe you *wouldn't* be in Heaven." The thought just blurted out of me and it was the wrong thing to say. Harry's eyes went from sad to fearful. I stumbled through my words, trying to recover. "I mean, when you got older you weren't always a good man." I was getting myself in deeper, but I couldn't stop. "You weren't always a good father or a good husband or even a good friend."

"Why?" Harry screamed. "What did I do?"

I could tell that my comments had rekindled some smoldering guilt in my pal's memory.

"Look, Harry, I'm not going to answer that. Rockland boys don't spread rumors about other Rockland boys. None of us were angels. But if you believe in God, like you say you do," I tried to keep my voice calm, "then you have to believe there's a reason why your memory got wiped out. Maybe it's your chance to set things right."

"Was I really evil?" Harry looked shocked and afraid. "Was I like a devil?" It bothered me that he spoke about morality like a child, and I cringed to hear his childish gibberish.

"No. You weren't the devil," I stammered. "Basically you were a good man. You weren't abusive or anything. You just did some thoughtless things.

Sometimes you *used* your friends and you weren't always as respectful to your wife and family as you should have been."

"How thoughtless?" he shot back.

"You weren't bad, Harry. Not bad enough to..." I hesitated, then spoke the next words very deliberately. "Do you remember in grade school, when the nuns taught us about Purgatory?"

"Purgatory?" His voice was beginning to calm down. "No, what is it?"

I wasn't really that comfortable talking about God or the afterlife. But it was too late to turn back now. "They said it was a place where God sent people who weren't bad enough to go to Hell, but not quite good enough to go directly to Heaven. It was like this place where you went and suffered for a while, and after you paid for your sins, then you went to Heaven." Harry looked confused, but I pushed on. "But what if Purgatory's not a place up in the sky? What if *this* is Purgatory? Maybe you have to suffer here for a while and then you can go to Heaven."

Harry sat on the edge of the bathtub and put his face in his hands. "That makes sense," he whispered. "No one's suffering more than I am. But what did I ever do that was good? Tell me that. What did I do that would make God *ever* want me in Heaven?"

I immediately remembered an episode from 1964, from that same summer. But it was so complicated, so involved, I wasn't sure I could explain it. It was about fear and courage, about compassion and empathy, about dignity and pride. I had already upset him so much. I hesitated to push his damaged brain any further. So I sat there and said nothing.

"Teddy," Harry broke the silence. "Who was the Green Man?"

I felt a rush of adrenalin or something like it. The top of my head tingled and went weightless, like it might float away. My ears rang loudly, then faded to silence. He knew the story! Somehow he knew what I was going to say.

"The Green Man, Harry... the Green Man is how I know you're basically good. The Green Man is your ticket to Heaven!"

chapter eighteen

Green Man

We had worked hard during those two-a-day practices. It was the third week of July and the team was really beginning to jell. We had taken hundreds of rounds of infield and outfield practice, spent hours in the batting cage, and worked on the finer points of the game, like bunting and base running and lining up throws from the outfield. We got to know one another's strengths and weaknesses. We could anticipate who would be covering which base and in which situation. We had become a team.

Coach Gallo had scheduled a few exhibition games with some neighboring towns, like New Galilee, Big Beaver, and Shenango, and we had won them all. He even scheduled a game with the Rotary, the first-place team from the Ellwood City Little League. Of course, they weren't an all-star team. They were just one of ten teams in the Ellwood City league. But they were the best team in the league with some great players, and none of them could hit Dawson.

By mid-July we were 4–0 in exhibition play, with the suburban New Galilee Tournament less than a week away. We would be the defending champs in that tournament and we couldn't wait to start playing for real.

Every year, in the week before the start of the tournament, the town of New Galilee held their Firemen's Carnival. It included parades and fireworks and a huge midway with fantastic rides, great food, and spectacular game booths. There were other carnivals around, but nothing came close to the one in New Galilee. As kids, we saved up our allowances all summer to have the money to spend at the big event.

It was a Thursday night during carnival week, and Uncle Joe and Aunt Betty were taking their entire family to New Galilee for a fun evening. Tony and I had planned to meet our girlfriends at the carnival. "Maybe we'll get them away from their parents for a while," Tony had boasted, "and walk around the carnival grounds showing them off." I had nodded my agreement. It was going to be a big night. We were both sure of that!

Molly and Pam were driving out with Pam's family, while Tony, Harry, and I had planned to go with Tony's family. The problem was that Harry and I didn't really fit in the car full of DeVitos. We decided to walk to my house and beg my father to take us. If that didn't work, we would beg Harry's father.

After half an hour of urging and pleading, and with a little friendly persuasion from my mother, my dad agreed to drive us to the carnival. "It's only for an hour, boys," he warned. "I have to go to work tomorrow."

Harry went home to grab some money and get washed up. I changed my shirt, kissed my mom goodbye, and climbed into the front seat of my dad's car. When we stopped to pick up Harry, his father came out to the car with him.

"He has his own money," Clark Kirkland told my dad. "I don't want you buying him anything." My dad nodded, then got out of the car and had a private conversation with Clark. Harry and I just sat in the car wondering what they could possibly be talking about. They seemed solemn and serious and Harry's dad just kept nodding his head while my dad did most of the talking.

Finally he got back in the car and we headed west toward the Rockland-New Galilee road. The road was about ten miles long. It was narrow and winding and a little treacherous at night, although we still had about twenty minutes before sundown.

My father was the first to speak. "Maybe on the way back we'll see the Green Man." Harry and I looked at each other with excitement, fear, and more than a little anxiety. We both knew the legend.

There was a man, it was said, who walked the New Galilee road at night. He had no face! Just scar tissue where his eyes and nose had once been, and a distorted half-open mouth. His right arm was missing and in his left hand he carried a long twisted walking stick. He went out at night to avoid the public eye, to get a little exercise, and to claim his right to exist, no matter how hideous his appearance was.

People called him "Charlie No-Face" or "the Green Man," because many unsuspecting motorists thought they had seen something from outer space, an alien, "a green man from Mars."

Every evening, all summer long, people would come from miles around to try to catch a glimpse of him. Teenage boys would bring their girlfriends and drive the New Galilee road hunting for him, hoping their girls would hold on tight just at the thought of encountering the Green Man.

Many folks thought he was just a legend, but he was real all right. He was my grandmother's age, born around 1910. According to her, his real name was Ray Robinson and he became an early victim of the industrialization of Western Pennsylvania at the age of eight.

In 1919, he and some of his friends were crossing the railroad bridge between Rockland and Big Beaver. The bridge was for trains only and foot traffic was forbidden. For that reason, the utility companies decided to lease space from the railroad to use the bridge to carry electrical power into the Rockland area. Only railroad and electric company workers were allowed on the structure.

There were tracks and generators and relays and huge high-voltage wires running across the bridge, not to mention the regular trolley trains. Parents warned their children to stay away, but kids knew a good shortcut when they saw it. It was a full fifteen minutes shorter to run over the railroad bridge than to cross the footbridge half a mile down the road.

Ray and his buddies were running the rails across the bridge when the eight-year-old lost his balance and toppled into the exposed power lines that ran the length of the structure. Instantly his little body crackled and burned on the high-voltage cables. His terrified friends ran for help as the smell of smoke and burning flesh filled the air.

By the time rescue workers arrived the boy was burned over ninety percent of his body and was barely alive. The newspapers of the day called the electrocution a devastating accident and immediately called for the removal of all high-voltage wires from areas accessible to the public. Doctors said the boy would be dead within twenty-four hours. They called him a "martyr" to public safety and said that his death would force reforms of the county's dangerous electrical grid.

"Hello, Ray," my father called out as we stood before him. Harry and my dad stood about a foot closer than I did. "My boys wanted to meet you."

A deep, muffled, faraway sound came from the direction of the Green Man's twisted, lip-less mouth. It sounded like "Hello, fellows," but I couldn't be sure.

My hands were shaking, my heart was pounding, and my mouth was dry. As hard as I tried, I couldn't speak. "Say something," my dad instructed, but I just couldn't.

"How about those Pirates?" Harry offered finally, his voice cracking with every word.

"Hey hink!" blurted out the figure in the dark.

Harry broke into laughter. "No, they don't stink. They're just having a bad month. With Clemente and Maz and Billy Virdon, they'll be back in September. You just wait and see."

My dad and I looked at Harry in amazement. He never seemed very mature before and he certainly never seemed particularly kind or compassionate. We were blown away.

"*We* play baseball," continued Harry. "We play for Rockland."

"And we're pretty good too," I chimed in.

The Green Man mumbled something I couldn't quite understand, but Harry and my dad both laughed out loud. "Maybe we *could* help the Pirates," Harry answered. And we all laughed again.

"Well, I've got to get these boys home, Ray," my dad said in a measured, confident voice, as he put his hands on our shoulders. "Thank you for talking with us."

"Fine boys," said the Green Man, clear as a bell. "Fine boys."

My father was always proud of my ball playing, proud of my good grades and proper manners. But he was never as proud as he was that night. And it was Harry who made it possible. He overcame his own fear. He saw a human being, not a monster. He saw a tortured soul and treated him with dignity.

And even though Harry was only twelve years old, he was already a good man.

chapter nineteen

The Only Thing That Matters

"Is that for real?" Harry asked as he turned away from his own reflection and walked back into the hospital room. "I thought I remembered a man with no face, but I figured it was just a movie or something."

"Ray Robinson was real all right," I assured him. "We both stood in front of him; talked to him. It was the worst disfigurement I ever saw, worse than anything in the movies. And he had to live like that for sixty-five years: no friends, no joy, just suffering."

"He'd have been better off dying," Harry sighed, studying my face for a reaction.

"Maybe," I responded, "but it wasn't really his choice to make, was it? Anyway, he's gone now. He passed away in 1985." I waited for the question I knew was coming.

"Do you think he's in Heaven, Teddy?"

"If anybody's in Heaven, he is." I paused for a long moment to let my answer sink in. I wasn't sure if Harry would see the correlation.

"So I talked with him," Harry continued, shifting the subject slightly. "I was nice to him. Do you really think God cares about that? I mean, do you really think it matters?"

"Yes, I do," I said, as I sank back into the fake-leather chair in the corner. "I think it's the *only* thing that matters."

Harry stood silently for what seemed like five minutes. Finally he walked over to the window and looked out through the bars into the green courtyard with its hedges and trees and shadows. "You know, this isn't really such a bad place," he sighed as he turned around to look at me. And for some reason we both started laughing—loud, long, hysterical laughter. As usual, Harry laughed until he cried. But this time, my eyes welled up too.

We were both still chuckling when we were interrupted by a loud banging at the door. "Harry, I need to come in," shouted big James from the hallway.

"Go away," Harry barked back. "This is private."

"I have to piss really bad," screamed his roommate with obvious panic in his voice. Harry walked over and opened the unlocked door.

"Hurry up, then," he ordered as the big man scurried past him.

Harry sat back on the bed and smiled while James urinated for what seemed like ten minutes. "Christ," Harry smirked. "He wasn't kidding."

I felt a wave of well-being pass over me. It was like we were kids again— same cocky attitude, same wise-ass comments. I didn't know how much he would remember, or how long it would last. But I was sure of one thing: my buddy was back!

"So how did we do in New Galilee?" His mind was running ahead of me now.

"What do you mean?" I asked, trying to catch up.

"The tournament," he continued. "How did we do in the New Galilee Tournament?"

"It had its ups and downs," I responded, and I eagerly began recounting the details of the story he once knew like the back of his hand.

chapter twenty

"Get an Out"

We opened the New Galilee Tournament on Saturday with an easy 8–0 victory over West Mayfield. Dawson surrendered only one hit and struck out sixteen batters. This was an amazing total, considering that Little League games are only six innings long and there are only eighteen outs to get. The other two outs came from West Mayfield batters, who were so frustrated they tried to bunt their way on base. One bunted toward Ray Marino at third. The other bunted to Tony at first. As the second baseman, I covered first base on both plays and recorded both putouts. This is something we practiced about five hundred times during our two-a-day practices in July and we handled each bunt as just another routine play.

It was a little hard to concentrate on the game while Dawson just plowed through the weak West Mayfield lineup, but we were taught to always know what to do with the ball if it was hit to us, so most of my time in the field was spent waiting and worrying about what I would do if the ball was hit my way, even though it never was. It's a unique kind of mental anguish that infielders know better than anyone else.

About 150 Rockland fans showed up for the game, including Pam and Molly and all the neighborhood girls. Pam came to every game, while Molly, as a ten-year-old, was only allowed to come to every other game. I'm sure it was some sort of compromise she had worked out with her protective parents.

My mom was in top form that day, cheering my name every time I came to bat and screaming at the umpires every time a close call went against us.

She wasn't the only mother who shrieked and screamed on every play. Janie Kirkland would rain sarcasm down on every umpire and opposing coach and even some of the opposing players. She seemed to know everyone's name, but only their *last* name. "That's right, Spillman," I once heard her shout at an Elwood City pitcher who had just beaned her son, "We see you smiling out there. We know you threw at him!" And Joanie Bruno, Skip's mom, roared like a tiger and seemed like she was ready to curse at any time, but she almost never did.

Billie Conti's mother was the Irish bride his dad brought home from the war. "Are ya' blind or sumthin'?" Agnes Conti would scream at the umpires in her thick Irish brogue after almost every pitch that was called against us. All the ballplayers were a little embarrassed at the antics of our mothers, but their love and devotion was never in question. And although we rolled our eyes, it was comforting in a way to hear their outrageous comments.

But of course it was Aunt Betty who was the star of the show. Her particular point of view was that our runners were always safe, our pitchers threw only strikes, our boys were always heroes, and that the umpire and the opposing coach were somehow linked in a conspiracy against us. She was constantly outraged and argumentative and she kind of guided the psyche of our whole fan base. Plus, her comments were hilarious. "Hey, tub o' lard," she once screamed at a particularly stout umpire. "You can't see the play from here. You gotta waddle over there to make that call." The fans at a Rockland game formed their own little society and Aunt Betty was their queen.

The fathers weren't as demonstrative as the mothers, but they were just as dedicated. All the steelworker fathers who were working weekend shifts had either traded work times with someone who didn't have a son on the team or had simply called off sick so they could attend the game. Ray and Terry Marino's dad, "Nip" Marino, had obviously called off work. He wore dark sunglasses and sat alone on a lawn chair way down the first-base line so nobody would recognize him.

I had a base hit in the first inning and knocked in our second run of the game. I also drew a walk later and scored our fifth run. So I didn't mind when Coach Gallo let Terry Marino pinch-hit for me late in the game. After all, we already had an eight-run lead and Dawson was cruising through the West Mayfield lineup.

Terry, a ten-year-old like me, singled sharply to left field to start the fifth inning and stood proudly at first base, grinning from ear to ear. Instantly, his dad blew his cover by standing and cheering, "Atta' baby… That's my boy… That's my boy." All the Rockland fans laughed and shook their heads when they recognized Nip.

After the game, I spent a few minutes talking to Molly and playfully fitted my baseball cap on her head as she walked me to my parents' car for the ride back to Rockland. She really looked great with that hat tilted back and her long, soft hair shining in the August sun. When we got to the car, she asked my mom for a pen, then wrote her name on the inside brim of the hat. Right underneath her name she added a little heart. Man, I was crazy about that girl.

On Wednesday at 6 p.m., we were back in New Galilee to face Enon Valley, one of three Ohio teams in the tournament. On four days' rest, Derrick Dawson was again on the mound, striking out fourteen and pitching his second shutout of the week. We won the game 5–0 and I had a single in my second-straight tournament game. Dawson also homered in the game and Tony had two hits.

In the fifth inning, Harry drove a ball deep into center field, where an Enon Valley outfielder went back to the warning track and leaped high over the wall to make the catch. It was an amazing drive, but Harry was heartbroken.

There were only a couple guys on our team who could hit the ball deep on a regular basis. The rest of us were singles hitters. A home run would have been a dream come true for Harry. Instead he hit a deep fly that would be forgotten an hour later. I felt bad for him.

Still the Rockland All-Stars rolled on. There were sixteen teams in the New Galilee Tournament, and after two victories, we had reached the semifinals of the single-elimination event.

On the following Saturday we returned to New Galilee to face Highland. They were a solid team from just outside of Beaver Falls. Like Rockland, they were fiercely independent, and although they had been invited to join the Beaver Falls Little League, they instead had put together their own competitive four-team league. Their all-star team was well-coached and talented.

This time on just three days' rest, Dawson returned to the mound. We knew he couldn't pitch every day, and the championship game was scheduled for Sunday, the very *next* day. But Highland looked to be the strongest of the three remaining teams, so Coach Gallo decided to start Derrick in the semifinal game and take our chances with Tony or Will DeLuca pitching the championship game.

Nearly 300 Rockland fans showed up for the game. With two outs in the first inning, Beans Baruby doubled down the third-base line. The Highland coach intentionally walked Dawson. Then big Ricky Baldwin also walked on six pitches. That brought me to the plate with two outs and the bases loaded. I was scared shitless.

I could hear everyone I knew in the stands: my dad, my brother, my girlfriend, the neighborhood kids, and of course my mom. But I didn't dare look at any of them. I was too nervous already, and seeing their faces would have made it worse. I stepped out of the batter's box and looked at the third-base coach. He was flashing me the *take* sign, meaning I wasn't supposed to swing until I had a strike on me.

I hated giving up the plate, but I dutifully watched the first pitch come right down the middle for strike one. The Highland pitcher, Brian Carlson, then tried to hit the outside corner with the next two pitches, but they were both called balls.

I knew this was my best shot. With the bases loaded, I knew Carlson wouldn't want to throw another ball. I also figured he wouldn't take a chance on his curveball. I waited for a fastball down the middle, and the Highland starter didn't disappoint me. I lined the pitch up the middle for a base hit. Beans scored easily from third, but when Dawson tried to score from second, the Highland centerfielder threw him out at the plate.

As we took the field for the second inning I could still hear the cheers ringing in my head. I looked into the stands and saw my family and friends beaming back at me. I remember thinking that, for the first time, I was really an important member of this team. Sure, I had made a few good plays in the field and had a couple decent hits, but I hadn't really done anything important until now. Who knows? Maybe we would win 1–0 and my hit would decide the game.

The score remained the same until the bottom of the fourth inning, when Will DeLuca doubled in our second run. Then Dawson hit a three-run homer to push the score to 5–0. In the field, we were playing our third errorless game of the tournament.

In the bottom of the fifth, we scored our sixth run, and figured the game was all but over. But in the top of the sixth and final inning, Highland finally got to Dawson. The first two batters both singled and then Ray booted a ground ball at third to load the bases.

"Infield up," shouted Harry to the rest of the infielders. "Cut down the runner at the plate."

"No, no," barked Jiggy from the dugout. "We're ahead 6–0. Play back. Just get the out. Get *any* out at *any* base."

The Highland cleanup hitter came to the plate and immediately hit a sharp ground ball between first and second. I moved quickly to my left and knocked down the ball, throwing out the runner at first. Dawson had given up his first run of the tournament, and Highland still had runners on second and third and only one out.

The next hitter bounced a ground ball to Harry at shortstop. He calmly fielded the ball and threw to first for the second out, as Highland scored their second run.

Now Highland had a runner at third with two outs. Dawson then reached back and threw three fastballs past the next batter, who swung at all three pitches but didn't get close to any of them. We were on our way to the championship game with the 6–2 victory. And the Rockland fans screamed their approval.

Harry sought out Dawson after the game. "I'm sorry you lost the shutout," he told the big left-hander as we walked off the field. "We should have played with the infield up and got the runner at home, but Jiggy made us play back. That loudmouth thinks he knows everything."

I saw Coach Gallo coming way before Harry did. He had overheard the comment and could hardly contain his anger. "Kirkland!" he screamed. "Wait in the dugout until everyone's gone."

"Why?" Harry answered back, digging his grave a little deeper.

"You punk," shouted Johnny. "You think you know more than the coaching staff? Jiggy DeVito's *forgotten* more about this game than you'll *ever* hope to know. Now sit down and shut up and maybe I'll keep you on this team!"

I had a strange feeling walking toward the Rockland fans waiting in the bleachers—all those happy faces: my mom, my dad, Molly, smiling and sweet. But all I could think of was Harry, and as I passed the stands I tried to avoid looking into his parents' eyes while they waited for their son to exit the dugout. "Let *him* explain it to them," I thought, as I turned away from the Kirklands' happy, glowing faces.

Finally Harry came out of the dugout and started walking toward us. Tony and I ran up to meet him halfway. "What happened?" Tony whispered as we closed in on our shortstop.

"They're benching me for the championship game," Harry sobbed without looking up from the ground.

"Who's going to play short?" Tony gasped. Harry just shook his head and said nothing as he walked slowly toward his family.

Tony and I looked at each other without a word. It was the worst punishment I could ever imagine. I would rather have had a hundred whacks with the belt than miss the championship game. No, *five* hundred whacks. It was the worst thing that could ever happen to a Rockland boy.

We watched Harry approach his parents, looking grave and concerned. He started speaking but never lifted his eyes from the ground. His father, who sometimes helped Jiggy coach our Board of Trade team, took off his hat and slammed it to the ground. "How could you be so stupid?" he screamed at Harry. "We were leading 6–0 with the bases loaded, of course you play for the out. That runner at third meant nothing. Nothing! And to *question* the coaches. What's the matter with you?"

It was a typical response. In 1964 our parents always sided with our coaches or teachers or even with other parents. We were taught to respect authority and it was rare for any father to side with his son against any authority figure. It was probably a military thing. Who knows?

"He brought it on himself," Tony muttered to me as we watched from a distance. But I felt empty and nauseous, and I couldn't even speak. "Who's going to play short?" he continued. "And Dawson can't throw tomorrow. We need to be at our best. Harry might have just cost us the tournament."

We walked back toward the stands. "Uncle Joe and Johnny are going to stay and watch the next game," my father shouted brightly. I figured he didn't know about Harry. "Do you want to come home with us or stay and watch Bessemer and New Galilee?"

The other two semifinal teams were now taking the field, and we would be facing the winner the next day for the tournament championship. "I guess I'll stay," I told him, although I didn't really want to stay.

I was worried about Harry but I didn't want to disappoint the coaches. They would be scouting the game and offering us tips on how to defend against our next opponent. I should have been excited that they wanted me to be there, but just for one moment, I felt a little resentful of their authority. Then it was gone.

The Bessemer team looked strong, but New Galilee, the host team, seemed to get every close call. It's not that the umpires were openly dishonest. They just seemed to be making a lot of calls with their hearts instead of their eyes. The score was 5–5 as the final inning started, and the dark clouds that had been threatening throughout the game finally opened into a slow-but-steady rain.

Bessemer got the first two runners on base in the top of the sixth, but the New Galilee pitcher got the next two batters on strikes. Then, with two outs, a kid named Hardy drove a pitch deep into the dark skies, putting Bessemer up by three runs. New Galilee went down one-two-three in the bottom of the sixth, to the dismay of the home crowd.

As we headed back to the car, a huge bolt of lightning lit up the sky and a clap of thunder shook the ground. It started raining so hard that we could barely see as we made our way back along the treacherous Rockland-New Galilee road.

The next morning, I got a call from Johnny Gallo at about ten a.m. Our championship game against Bessemer had been rained out and postponed until the following Sunday. Dawson would get all the rest he needed to pitch the final. We seemed destined to win the tournament.

chapter twenty-one

Why Me?

I stopped my storytelling for a moment because the pale-green room at Mayview Hospital had grown very quiet. "Harry, are you all right?" As before, he was looking out into the courtyard, but now he wasn't focused on anything in particular. He just stared out the window vacantly. "Harry… Harry, say something," I repeated, but it was like I wasn't even there.

Suddenly a banging on the door broke the silence and the pastel nurse entered the room, followed by an orderly pushing a meds cart. "I have your medication, Mr. Kirkland." Her tone was very businesslike and I could tell she was still unnerved by Harry's earlier comments.

"OK," he sighed in an almost inaudible voice, and he shuffled across the room to where she stood. It was like someone had squeezed the juice out of a lemon. Harry just stood there, limp and pale and fragile. The nurse sensed his change in demeanor immediately and seemed pleased to be back in her comfort zone. She launched back into her customary jolly self. "Can you take these for me?" she sang, handing him a tiny plastic cup with three or four pills at the bottom.

Harry obligingly took the plastic container and tipped the pills into his mouth. Then he took a Dixie cup filled with water and chased down the mouthful of medication.

"Open wide, please," the nurse sang out again. And Harry obediently opened his mouth while she inspected his teeth and gums and under his tongue to make sure he wasn't hiding any tablets.

"You've gotta be shitting me," I said under my breath, but loud enough for her to hear. She turned and looked me straight in the eye. Then smiled that gargoyle smile and left the room. The zombie orderly followed close behind her pushing the cart, and we listened to it rattle down the hall until the room grew silent again.

"Harry," I repeated. "Are you OK?" But he wouldn't even look my way and I wasn't sure whether he was reacting to my story or had just lapsed into some kind of mental dysfunction. "Is there anything I can do?" I was beginning to worry now. "Do you want me to get a doctor?"

Harry just kept shaking his head. "Why me?" he whispered finally. "Why does everything happen to me?" And I realized he was reliving one of the worst moments of his life. "A Little-League tournament," he rambled. "I can't have that. I can't even have that! Did we lose the tournament?" He looked at me like a dog that just got caught pissing on the sofa. "Was it my fault?"

I felt a little relief that he wasn't completely catatonic, but now I realized that my words had caused his depressive behavior and I wondered how I could finish my story without upsetting him again. How could I talk about the good times without referring to the bad times? How could I explain the highs without mentioning the lows?

"Harry," I said in an even, measured voice. "The story's far from over. Why don't you wait to see how it all comes out?"

Harry nodded and I slowly launched back into my memories of 1964. But this time I reminded myself that I was speaking to a frail, damaged human being, and it would take more than one afternoon of reminiscing to restore his crushed ego and broken soul.

chapter twenty-two

That's Justice

The postponement of the New Galilee championship game helped us in one respect: we could start Derrick Dawson in the final of the suburban tournament. But it certainly hurt our chances in the big New Castle Tournament. That battle would start on Wednesday, and although there was a good chance no games would be scheduled simultaneously, it still would be a big drain on our pitching staff to throw in two tournaments in the same week.

The New Castle Tournament was the premier Little-League event in Western Pennsylvania and Eastern Ohio. There were twenty-eight teams entered in the double-elimination tournament, which took nearly three weeks to complete. All the big cities had one or two teams entered, and all the best players in a fifty-mile radius would be there.

It was played in Little-League heaven, Dean Park in New Castle, which was built to resemble Forbes Field, the home of the Pittsburgh Pirates. It was green and plush with a beautifully groomed infield and well-trimmed outfield. It was surrounded by a warning track and a four-foot-high green wall. It featured a state-of-the-art electronic scoreboard in left field.

The dugouts were built about two feet below ground level, with padded benches and green wire screens across the front to protect the players from foul balls. The seating was like a Major League stadium, with individual box seats behind home plate and permanent bleacher seats built into the hillside surrounding the first- and third-base lines.

It was a near-perfect miniature version of old Forbes Field, and it took my breath away every time I saw it.

We opened the New Castle Tournament against one of the host teams, the New Castle Americans. Even though Dawson had to pitch our championship game against Bessemer on Sunday, the coaching staff figured he could start this Wednesday game and still have four days' rest before throwing in New Galilee.

Although New Castle had one of the best Little-League programs in the state, we weren't really intimidated by this *Americans* team. There were a lot of big programs around, but each city handled its all-star selection differently. In Ellwood City, they had so many good ballplayers that they would select *two* equally matched all-star teams. In Beaver Falls, they had sixteen Little League teams to choose from, but decided to field only one very strong all-star team. In New Castle, they choose two teams, but put all the best players on the Nationals. The second-tier all-stars would play for the Americans.

Still, they were a big-city team, and I'm sure the New Castle tournament directors thought they were feeding the Americans an easy victory over tiny Rockland in the first round.

The directors were in for a surprise. Dawson shut out the Americans on just two hits. He struck out thirteen and we played great defense behind him. In fact, Beans threw out both runners trying to steal second.

It was the first time I went hitless, but it didn't matter. Will DeLuca hit a two-run homer in the first inning and we coasted to a 4–0 victory. Surprisingly, Harry started at shortstop. The coaches made it clear that, as his punishment, he would still be benched for the New Galilee Tournament Championship but was considered a "hustling, hardworking member of our team," and was still our starting shortstop. Harry responded with two singles against the Americans, and he and Tony were both cited for their "sparkling defensive play" by the *New Castle News*, the local paper that reported on every game.

The New Castle Americans were a good test for us. They weren't the best players in the city, but they *were* big—a lot bigger physically than we were. And they shouted and threatened and tried to intimidate us on every ground ball we fielded and every pitch we faced. Even their coach seemed to encourage their taunting. It was Bush League all the way around. Their intimidation tactics finally came to a head in the bottom of the fifth.

With one out, Dawson walked the second batter, a tough, loud-mouthed Irish shortstop named Hanlan. You could tell the kid had talent, but he seemed to lose his temper on every close play.

The next batter hit a ground ball toward Harry at short and I ran over to cover second base for the double play. But when Harry bobbled the ball, I decided to just take the force out at second. It would be too late to get the runner at first.

I took the throw at second base then stepped toward the outfield side of the bag to avoid the sliding runner. Except he didn't slide; he ran straight through the bag and knocked me to the ground behind second base. He caught me with an elbow to the chin and my head banged hard against the infield clay.

I lay there in a daze until I heard the coaches and umpires standing over me. Dawson and all our infielders were crowded around me, and Uncle Joe was pulling up and down on my belt to make sure I was breathing normally. Johnny Gallo was screaming at the umpires and the opposing coach. "That's interference," he insisted. "He's supposed to slide. The runner at first should be out too. In fact, that kid should be thrown out of the game."

"Bullshit!" screamed the New Castle coach. "The collision wasn't intentional." But everyone could see that it was. The tournament umpires had been hired by the host team, and although they seemed to sympathize with Coach Gallo's argument, it was clear that we *weren't* going to get the out at first base and *nobody* was going to get thrown out of the game.

Then the New Castle coach added insult to injury. "What's the call at second?" he demanded smugly, looking around for the ball, "I never heard a call on the play at second base."

I was still lying on my back with Jiggy checking my injuries. My shoulder ached and my head was ringing from the collision, but I held up my glove with the ball still locked in the pocket. "Out!" barked the ump, "definitely out."

Johnny Gallo glared at the opposing coach and umpire as they walked together back toward home plate. Then he and Jiggy helped me off the field, while Dawson followed close behind. "Nice Play, Teddy," Derrick said, tapping me on the shoulder with his glove.

"Lefty," Coach Gallo whispered as Terry Marino ran out to replace me at second base, "take care of this." Dawson nodded, and headed for the mound, but his sleepy eyes and emotionless expression never changed.

When I reached the dugout, I held an icepack to the lump on my head and sat on the bench trying to get my bearings. "Teddy," grunted Uncle Joe, "you made a great play out there. I'm proud of you."

"Thanks," I answered. But he could tell I was upset. As the only ten-year-old I was an easy target for bullies and assholes, and this was the first time I was playing outside the protection of Rockland Little-League officials. It was like I was wounded in battle, except there was no pride in it.

"Come here for a second," he said, grabbing me by the sleeve and pulling me toward the dugout screen. "Watch."

Dawson went into his windup now and fired a high inside pitch to the next New Castle batter. "Thud!" It was a sickening collision of horsehide and human ribs. "Ughhh!" screamed the batter as he flopped around on the ground like a giant mackerel. He was gasping for air and moaning in pain.

"That's justice," whispered Jiggy as he slapped me on the back. "The thugs will always try to turn the game into a street fight, but baseball has its own rules. It's like a battlefield between those lines. If you want to fight them, fight them out there. Whoever wins the game wins the war. They'll try to humiliate you with words and threats, but there's nothing more humiliating than defeat."

The umpires never even issued a warning to Dawson. I think they considered his actions justified payback. The next hitter was terrified out of his mind. He swung wildly at three pitches and sat down. They never got another man on base.

There was an added benefit to beating the New Castle Americans in the opening round: we inherited their easy schedule. There were twenty-eight teams in the tournament. That meant fourteen first-round winners, so two teams would get a bye in the second round. The New Castle tournament officials had done their best to get their second-tier all-stars into the third round by setting them up to get a second-round bye. But when we knocked them off, we took their place in the brackets and got a free trip to the quarter-finals.

The day after the New Castle game we were back on the practice field, feeling every bit a championship-caliber team. On Thursday we worked on the fundamentals—fifteen rounds of infield and outfield practice—followed by an hour of batting practice. As each player entered the batter's box he had to bunt five consecutive pitches before he was allowed to swing away.

On Friday word came out that Bessemer had knocked off New Brighton in the second round of the New Castle Tournament. This was a huge upset. Bessemer, like Rockland, was a small suburban team, while New Brighton, with a great sports heritage, was the home of current Major-Leaguer Tito Francona and future Major-League player Terry Francona. It was one of the biggest towns around and they had a great program. Their loss to Bessemer was good news to us. The air of invincibility surrounding the city teams was beginning to deteriorate.

The victory affected us directly too, because now Bessemer, whom we would battle for the New Galilee suburban championship on Sunday, would also be our third-round opponent in the New Castle Tournament on the following Tuesday.

As our Friday-afternoon practice session came to an end, Coach Gallo called us into the dugout for his daily assessment of our progress and work habits. "We're playing pretty good ball right now, boys." He looked up and down the bench. "And we're right where we want to be."

"We've got Bessemer on Sunday for the New Galilee title, and then we play them again on Tuesday in the quarter-finals in New Castle. Of course, Derrick can't pitch *both* games so we've decided to use him in the title game."

I had mixed emotions regarding the announcement. We had won the suburban tournament in '63, and although it was a great morale-booster for the town of Rockland, it didn't compare to the tournament in New Castle, where the competition was unrestricted and where no Rockland team had ever won more than two games.

"If we keep winning in New Castle, all well and good," shrugged Johnny, "but we're going to concentrate on winning the New Galilee Tournament first. Besides," he continued, "they give nicer trophies anyway."

As hard as I tried not to, I instinctively rolled my eyes. While the New Galilee trophies might look nicer than the New Castle trophies, there was no question which one we would rather win. Still, as I looked around the dugout, almost everyone was nodding their heads in agreement with what the coach had just said.

"I agree with him," Tony replied as I questioned him on our walk home after practice. "So do I," nodded Harry. "Why should we have come this far and go home empty-handed?"

"But to win in New Castle," I wondered out loud, "would be the ultimate victory."

"I say, get the New Galilee trophies first, then we'll work on New Castle," Harry responded.

"Who cares about trophies?" I deadpanned. And everybody broke into laughter. The fact is, we *all* cared about trophies. We cared because almost no one ever got one. In those days, the Rockland Little League never gave out trophies for our local playoffs or regular season. If there was any money left from fundraising it went to buying equipment or uniforms. It wasn't wasted on trophies.

The trophies we won in the 1963 New Galilee tournament were the first ones ever taken home by Rockland boys. Mine sat by itself in a place of honor atop the black-and-white Westinghouse TV in our living room. I didn't want to end 1964 without a companion for it, but the prestige of winning in New Castle is something that could follow a player for years.

"It doesn't matter what we think anyhow," Tony argued. "The decision has already been made."

And so it had.

When I got home from practice, Nelson and my little sister Sophie were lying in front of the TV with their heads on pillows watching *Huckleberry Hound*. "Poor Nelson," I thought. "He must be bored out of his mind." Ever since all-star practice had started, I hadn't seen much of Nelson and my dad had warned me that I needed to pay more attention to my brother.

"The floor is acid!" I shouted as I entered the living room. Nelson picked up on my cue immediately and knew the game was on. He leaped from the floor to the safety of the couch, while Sophie, who was about six years old, rolled around on the rug screaming in mock pain. Finally she sat up on her pillow. "I guess I'm dead," she said dryly, and turned her attention back to her cartoons.

But Nelson was ready for fantasy. "Step on those pillows, and then hop up on the couch," he instructed. I jumped the six feet from pillow A to pillow B, but my momentum forced me to put a foot down on the rug.

"The floor is acid," screamed Nelson. "Your foot is gone." And I groaned in pain. "You have to hop now," he continued.

I leaped from the second pillow to the couch, landing on my right knee and left "stump."

At first we played army buddies, trying to stay away from the enemy acid pit, but soon that got boring, so we became professional wrestlers and began pushing each other's appendages into the liquid death that surrounded the sofa.

I was bigger than Nelson, so to make things fairer I allowed him to push my left hand onto the carpet while I pretended to fight back. "Your arm's gone," Nelson squealed. "Now you have one leg and one arm."

I figured that was enough of an advantage and began wrestling at full strength with my one good arm and one good leg. Within minutes I had pinned Nelson to the cushions, and he shouted and cursed as I slowly pushed his face toward the rug.

"What are you doing?" my mother screamed as she entered the room. She had been washing sheets in the basement and ran up the steps when she heard the racket. "Let go of your brother right now."

I started to release Nelson from my grip. But as soon as I did, he spun around on the couch and pushed me from behind. It took all my strength to keep from losing a second leg to the insidious acid. I held onto the inner springs of the sofa with my one good arm while Nelson pushed down on my head with all his strength. "Stop, stop this minute," my mother shrieked. "What's wrong with you kids?"

"Get him off of me!" I shouted toward my mother. I figured I could use this quote to defend myself later, when my dad got home and interrogated us. Meanwhile, I was slowly working my way back from the edge of the sofa.

"Stop this instant," my mother demanded, "or I'll tell your father when he gets home!"

I knew we were passing a point of no return here, but I had tried to stop once, and Nelson took advantage of the situation. I knew we'd get punished, but I'll be damned if I was losing another leg.

Once I got myself back on the couch, it wasn't long before I flipped Nelson down into the bubbling liquid. He screamed a long, agonizing death cry.

"We're done now," I shouted to my mom. But she had long since stormed out of the room. "Do you think she'll tell him?" Nelson looked worried. "Don't you?" I asked accusingly. "Why didn't you stop?"

"Why didn't *you* stop?" I could see Nelson formulating his own testimony for my dad's interrogation. We didn't say another word until my father got home at 5:15.

"Teddy pushed me in the acid," Nelson barked before my dad even got a foot in the door. "You started it," I answered automatically.

"No, he said the floor was acid."

"But *he* wouldn't stop when Mommy told us to."

My father moaned and rolled his eyes. "Can't I even get in the door?"

"These kids are driving me crazy," my mother injected as she flew in from the kitchen. And the trial was on. I gave my testimony and Nelson gave his. Like any good district attorney, my mom demanded justice.

My father held court for the next five minutes. The verdict was always the same: we would *both* get punished.

"Now do you know *why* you're getting this punishment?" my father questioned as he held his leather belt in his hand and prepared to apply the whacks. Corporal punishment wasn't good enough for my father. We had to *admit* our mistakes.

I wanted to say, "Yeah, because I played with my brother." But I couldn't let Nelson know that I didn't really *want* to play this stupid game. That was the only good thing that was going to come out of this mess; I had spent some time playing with Nelson. I wasn't going to mess that up just to avoid a few cracks with the belt. "Yes," I told my dad. "I didn't listen to Mommy."

My father must have realized what was going on. He ended up going easy on us: two quick whacks with the belt and he never even snapped his wrists. Two minutes later, we were seated around the table eating my mom's mashed potatoes and meatloaf. The conversation during dinner centered on the Little League all-star team, but Nelson didn't seem jealous at all. He even said he wanted to go to the championship game.

Sunday morning was a perfect August day.

We arrived in New Galilee at noon for the one o'clock game. We had actually met at the Rockland ball field at 10 a.m. to loosen up and take a quick round of batting practice, then hopped into the coaches' cars and headed out to the tournament. By the time we got to New Galilee we were loose and eager to get going. Harry was on the bench for the game and I was worried that I might have to move to shortstop. But the coaches put Terry Marino at short and left me at second. I had a slightly better arm than Terry, but I guess they figured the fewer players out of position the better.

At about 12:30 the tournament officials brought out the trophies and lined them up on two presentation tables right next to the announcers' booth. Inside the booth, two New Galilee fathers were testing the public-address system. They already had the starting lineups taped to their desk. When you're ten years old, there's nothing quite like the thrill of hearing your name called over the loudspeakers when you come to bat in a big tournament.

I jogged over to the tables after infield practice and checked out the trophies. The team trophies were beautiful and looked like gold, although I'm sure they were just painted lead. The champions' trophy was the most beautiful thing I had ever seen. And I wondered what it would look like in the window of DeVito's drugstore on Main Street in the middle of town.

DeVito's front window had showcased the 1963 trophy from August through December of last year. It was still there on November 22, when John Kennedy was gunned down in Dallas. It seemed like seeing it was the only thing that made anyone smile in the weeks and months that followed the assassination. And now we were in a position to keep those smiles there for another year.

The individual championship trophies were a little smaller than I expected. Nice, but nothing special. The runner-up trophies were tiny, and I wondered if I would really take any pride in placing one of those on my family TV.

"We've got to win this thing," I told Tony as the record player connected to the public-address system crackled out the last few lines of "The Star-Spangled Banner" sung by Perry Como. All the adults were singing out loud with the music, but most of the players were too busy taking in the sights and sounds and smells of the tournament crowd to actually sing. We just stood with our hats across our hearts and fidgeted.

"I don't want those runner-up trophies," I said out loud as we returned to the dugout.

"I wouldn't even take one home," Harry added.

Tony laughed, "It's *your* fault if we *do* lose." He was teasing Harry about being benched, but there was also a hint of resentment that he had screwed up and put us at risk. Of course, Harry wasn't in a joking mood. He just lowered his head.

Bessemer was coming off their big upset of New Brighton in the New Castle tournament. They had a nice team, but struggled to hit Dawson. We scored one run in the top of the third when Tony singled home Billie Conti, and still had a 1–0 lead in the top of the sixth.

After Beans Baruby and Will DeLuca singled to lead off the inning, Dawson doubled home both runners and I singled home Derrick with our fourth run. It was my fourth hit of the tournament and I was flying high. We added one more run to take a 5–0 lead into the bottom of the last inning.

Bessemer scrambled for one run in the sixth, but we were never in danger of losing the game. They *did* have five hits, just one less than us, and Dawson uncharacteristically walked four batters, but our defense was tough and they couldn't score until it was too late. The game ended 5–1. Terry Marino, subbing for Harry, turned in a great game at shortstop, making two nice plays to end the final inning.

When his last throw to first smacked into Tony's glove, a roar went up from the Rockland fans and we all converged on the mound, where Uncle Joe and Coach Gallo bounced Dawson on their shoulders. I wouldn't call it complete pandemonium. There's a little something missing when you're the favorite in a tournament. This celebration was more of a relief than a thrill.

No one was more relieved than Harry. If Terry had cost us the game at shortstop, Harry would have never forgiven himself. And we probably wouldn't have forgiven him either.

All the fans cheered wildly as each player went to the speakers' stand to receive his trophy. Then we piled back into about forty cars and headed toward home.

When the caravan carrying players and fans got back to Rockland, we headed straight to the parking lot of the Italian Club. Phone calls back to town had been made from the phone booth at the carnival grounds. And friends and relatives who had not been able to attend the game were told to meet us at the lot in twenty minutes.

As we drove past the club, about a dozen more cars fell into line behind us, and we all started honking our horns, flashing our lights, and hanging out the windows screaming. The procession made its way up and down every street and avenue in town, and people came out on their porches shouting, "Rockland, Rockland," as we drove by.

"We're the champs!" we shouted back, waving our trophies.

"We beat Bessemer, 5–1," Tony shouted down to old Nick Fratelli, who was walking up Oak Street carrying a big basket of freshly picked corn on the cob.

"Put some on the stove for me, Grandpa. I'm coming over," Harry laughed.

"We're all coming," Tony added. And Nick wondered for a minute if he might be serious.

The whole thing only lasted about fifteen minutes, but I can still close my eyes and hear the celebration and feel the pride.

chapter twenty-three

Echoes

Harry sat on his bed and closed his eyes tightly. I could see he was trying to remember—trying to hear the shouting and car horns; trying to see the smiles on the faces of the boys waving trophies out the windows. He looked up at me in emptiness and frustration.

"Here we are, Harry," I said, offering him the news clipping once again. "Here's what we looked like."

"We look happy," Harry sighed. "But it just makes me feel sad to see it now." And he pushed the news photo away.

"Not me," I admonished him. "It always makes me smile. In fact, I don't even need to see the picture. I carry that championship around with me every day. Maybe not as much as when we were kids, but it's still part of my identity."

"That's what I don't have," Harry mumbled. "I don't have an identity."

The simplicity of his statement jolted me. Harry was right. Without his memories, who was he? Just a brain-damaged, toothless old man in a pale-green room, surrounded by psychotics and schizophrenics? No wonder he was depressed. No wonder he looked like he was eighty. He was just sitting there waiting to die.

"Today you're going to get that back," I promised him. "I'm going to remind you who you are."

"Why?" Harry looked at me blankly.

"Because you *are* your memories," I sputtered.

"What difference does it make?" Harry lowered his head again. "I'll forget it all tomorrow."

"You might forget the details, but you won't forget the feeling. You won't forget what it feels like to be a champion," I urged him. "What are you feeling right now?"

"I don't know." He shook his head. "I'm glad we won the tournament. I'm bunt down the third-baseline. Again the pitcher and third-baseman converged on the bunt, but this time both players pulled away from a collision and nobody fielded the baseball. We had the bases loaded with nobody out.

Now Beans came to the plate again. He stepped out of the batter's box and looked down at Coach Gallo at third. Harry was sitting next to me on the bench. He caught a glimpse of the coach's signal. "Jesus," he whispered, "We're bunting again."

"They haven't fielded one yet!" I reminded him.

Beans's bunt came straight back to the mound, but the pitcher bobbled it, then hurriedly tried to shovel the ball toward home. It sailed over the catcher's head and straight toward the backstop. The runner from third scored easily. So did the runner from second. And when the catcher's throw from the backstop bounced past the pitcher who was covering home plate, Tony hustled home all the way from first. We had a 6–5 lead.

"Incredible," chuckled Harry. "That team just fell apart on three bunts."

"Now you know why we spend so much time on fundamentals," barked Uncle Joe from the bench. "Sometimes you just have to put the ball in play."

I thought about the thousand rounds of infield. I thought about the hours we spent fielding bunts and practicing base running. I was starting to see the difference between us and everybody else. We weren't just all stars; we were an all-star *team*.

Tony shut down Bessemer in the bottom of the sixth with two ground balls to me at second base and then a bouncer up the middle that Harry fielded behind the bag and threw to Dawson, who had moved to first base when Tony came in to pitch. We had a hard-fought 6–5 victory, and Derrick Dawson never set foot on the mound.

We hustled off the field, slapping hands and shouting congratulations, then, as the lights came on for the night game, watched as Beaver Falls and Struthers, Ohio, took the field for pre-game warm-ups for *their* third-round contest.

There's always a two- to three-minute social phenomenon that takes place in baseball tournaments as one team leaves the dugout and the team playing the next game enters. There is minimal conversation, but a lot of focus on each word. Of course, it's always better for the exiting team if they won their game. You don't have to take any crap if you're coming off a victory.

Still, the Beaver Falls boys who were taking over our bench never congratulated us on our win. And a few of them made snide remarks about the size of our players. One claimed they would pound us in the final round. And another went so far as to say that Dawson was the only one on the Rockland team who could even make the Beaver Falls roster.

Harry heard the remark and glanced over at the Struthers, Ohio team warming up on the other side of the field. They all seemed to be nearly six feet tall. They were muscular and athletic and confident. They were all black.

"Aren't you getting a little ahead of yourself?" Harry cautioned. "You won't see us unless you beat these guys." And he nodded his head toward the Ohio team.

"We'll win our game!" offered a tall, left-handed Beaver Falls first-baseman. He pushed past Tony to take a seat on the bench.

"I hope you do," Tony shot back. "We'd rather face this team than that one."

The first-baseman took a step forward, and so did a tough-looking kid in shin guards and a chest protector. They outweighed us by about twenty-five pounds per man, but Tony wasn't worried about a fight. The adults were in charge here.

Uncle Joe, who had been collecting the warm-up balls and tossing them into a canvas bag, overheard the conversation. "Let's move on, boys," he barked at the Rockland team, then turned to the Beaver Falls team. "No need for talk, boys. You'll be getting all you want of these guys on the field."

And silence fell over the dugout as Jiggy strode off toward the gate behind home plate.

We walked off smiling. Harry had instigated the confrontation and Tony had held his own. And he was right; of course, we were already in the semifinals of the winner's bracket. They still had to play their way in. The first verbal volley of the tournament had been tossed and no one seemed intimidated by this powerful Beaver Falls team.

"What happens if Struthers does win?" Harry whispered to Tony and me as a single during a second-inning rally. After collecting four hits in the New Galilee suburban tournament, I finally had my first hit in the tough New Castle tournament. I was on top of the world.

The stage was set for the finals of the winners' bracket. We would be going head-to-head with the powerful Beaver Falls team on Monday night, just two days away, too soon for Dawson to pitch again. To win we'd have to do two things: we would have to play better than we ever played before, and we would have to do it without Derrick Dawson on the mound. The task seemed impossible.

chapter twenty-five

"Undefeated!"

Harry paced around his room, circling between the beds and around the fake-leather chair. "You're not going to tell me we beat them, are you? You're not going to say somebody stepped up and pitched the game of his life? No, no, Dawson was the only one who had a chance. How could we possibly win with anybody else on the mound?"

I chuckled and nodded. "Does this conversation sound familiar to you? We had this same discussion over thirty years ago. All of us. These are the same things we were saying then."

I could see it was coming back to him. First the fear and the intimidation, followed by the guts and determination. All the feelings we had all those years ago. Harry was having them now.

"Well, what happened? Did we win? How could we have won?" Harry couldn't contain his excitement. I realized that this was probably the first thing he had really cared about in a long time and I wasn't in any hurry to interrupt his emotions. I really wanted him to *feel* the story unwind.

"Slow down," I suggested. "Let me set the stage first. Remember, this was a *double* elimination tournament. That means we had to beat them twice."

"What?" screamed Harry. "That makes it even *more* impossible!"

I nodded my head in agreement. "If we lost this game we would drop down into the losers' bracket, then have to beat the winner of the New Castle–Ellwood City game, then come back and beat Beaver Falls twice to win the tournament."

"With our pitching staff?" Harry looked doubtful. "If we got knocked into the losers' bracket, there's no way we could have won that tournament."

"That's exactly what you said when you were twelve, Harry," I reminded him. "We were on our way to that Sunday practice, the day before the Beaver Falls game. It was the only time we ever practiced on Sunday. And half the town showed up to watch us take infield and batting practice. And the coaches were shouting and barking orders like drill sergeants. It was like we were heading for war. And you said that the only way to win the tournament was to go undefeated. And every time someone would make a great play during infield practice, you would yell, 'Undefeated, baby, undefeated!' We had to *talk it up* throughout infield anyway, and this was your little contribution to the infield chatter.

"All of a sudden, it caught fire and we all started barking 'Undefeated!' every time someone knocked down a line drive; 'Undefeated!' every time someone made a great throw or ran down a long fly ball. 'Undefeated!'

"During batting practice, the whole crowd got into it. Every hard-hit single or deep fly was greeted with 'Undefeated!' Half the town was there, shouting over and over again. And it was a Sunday, and it was just practice, but we felt unbeatable. You must remember that!"

"I don't remember the practice." Harry smiled at me. "But I remember the feeling."

"It was like we were playing for everyone in the town," I reminded him. "All those years of being second-class citizens. Even after going to war, even after rebuilding the economy, they still didn't feel like they really belonged. It had been years since anyone bragged about being from Rockland and we had a chance to change all that once and for all."

There was a long pause and we both sat in silence. I waited for him to speak next. He wrinkled his brow and seemed to be deep in thought, sorting through his emotions. "Teddy," he said finally. "Did your dad tell us a story that day, a war story?"

I felt my face turning red and my ears burning. "Holy shit, Harry, how did you remember that? I forgot that was the day. All the things our parents went through: the Great Depression, the bigotry, the Nazis, the war; it all seemed like ancient history to me, like something you read in a book. It wasn't *real* until that day, until we heard that story."

chapter twenty-six

Sons of the Atom Bomb

We were sitting on my back porch—Harry, Tony, my mom, my dad and me. And Tony was marveling over what had just happened at practice: more than 150 fans cheering every move we made, every routine ground ball we fielded, every fly ball our outfielders ran down. "Have you ever seen anything like that?" he asked, shaking his head.

My mom was serving us our second pitcher of Kool-Aid and the ice cubes were still swirling around in the plastic jug. It was a late Sunday afternoon in August, and the sky was just starting to darken behind the steel mill, which crackled and sizzled with the sound of molten steel hitting the molds.

"It doesn't surprise me," offered my father as he reached out with both his hands and grasped the clothesline that ran between the pillars of our back porch. He stood there like Atlas, arms stretched above his head as he watched the smoke rise from the factory, while the bright glow from the burning steel made the plumes flicker from white to orange and back again.

I remember thinking how solid he looked: strong but deep in thought as if he were watching all of history stretching out across our plush green lawn, over the spewing smoke and into the darkening sky. "You boys have no idea what you mean to this town."

I looked up at his face and for a moment I thought I saw tears welling up in his eyes. "Impossible," I thought. "I've never seen him cry in my life." I looked around at Tony and Harry and neither of them had seemed to notice. But my mom, barely five feet tall, crossed the porch and hugged him from behind, her big bosom pressed against his back. We all looked away, a little embarrassed. But my mother just kept squeezing him.

Harry kept his head down but was grinning from ear to ear, and Tony broke the silence with a quick chuckle he was unable to stifle.

chapter twenty-seven

The Weight

"Holy shit," moaned Harry, dropping his toothless face into his wrinkled hands. "That's a lot of responsibility to put on a bunch of kids."

I stared at Harry for a long time. I could hardly believe this was the same mumbling, washed-out old man who had stumbled down the hallway three hours ago.

"We were feeling the pressure. That's for sure." I told him. "My dad never mentioned the invasion of Japan again. But I guess he wanted us to know that we were part of something bigger than green backyards and playing Release and catching frogs. That we were standing on the shoulders of our parents and grandparents.

"We never faced the Depression. We never risked our lives at war. We never saw bigotry and injustice. I'm sure it was all around us, but our families shielded us from all of that.

"Now it was time for us to do our part; to finish the job; to grab back some of the dignity they had had yanked away from them while they were standing in line on Ellis Island."

"But my dad wasn't on those invasion ships," Harry winced. "He wasn't even in the Pacific."

"Your father parachuted into France," I reminded him, "Behind German lines! It's just as much of a miracle that he came home, back to this town, back to his little Italian girlfriend in Rockland."

"A miracle?" Harry jumped to his feet and stared me straight in the eyes. "So you think God saved them? You think God ended the war and brought them home?"

"I'm not sure," I answered, dropping my head. "How many innocent Japanese civilians died horrible deaths when we dropped those bombs? Fifty thousand… a hundred thousand… more? I just can't believe it was God's will for that to happen.

"I think my dad always felt a little guilty. Guilty that he lived while all those innocent people, all those women and children, died. But then, it wasn't his decision, was it? All he could do—all any of us can do—is to try to use our lives to make things better."

"And you think winning a baseball game was going to change the world?" Harry laughed.

"I don't know," I shrugged. "Maybe for some of the people in Rockland it would change the world. Maybe it would give them back something they didn't even know they had lost. Anyway, I know when we were sitting on my porch that night, watching the moon rise over the steel mill, that we felt the weight of the world on our shoulders. And nothing we had ever done before meant as much to us as that game."

"Are you going to tell me we won that game, Teddy? That without Dawson on the mound we went out and beat that unbeatable team?"

"Not exactly," I shrugged.

I remembered how quickly Harry had regressed when I mentioned his screw-up against Highland and his subsequent benching for the New Galilee championship game. I decided to proceed carefully with the story of our first battle against Beaver Falls.

chapter twenty-eight

Spahn and Sain

The last thing Coach Gallo had told us as we left that Sunday afternoon practice was to get a good night's sleep. "Go to bed early tonight," he suggested. "We need to be well-rested. We need to be at our best to beat Beaver Falls."

Still, the conversation on my back porch kept buzzing through my brain. I went to bed at nine o'clock and closed my eyes, but tossed and turned and twisted under the sheets for hours. I couldn't fully fall asleep. At best, it was a half sleep that incorporated things around me into my dreams… like the noise from a passing train, or the buzzing from the test pattern on the TV downstairs (after my dad had fallen asleep on the couch).

I dreamed I was running down the tracks… and a train was closing in on me… and a giant wasp landed in front of me, blocking my way. It was making this shrill humming sound. I awoke for ten seconds, turned my pillow over to the cool side, and slipped back into semi-consciousness. That's the way the whole night passed. I woke up red-eyed and yawning. *I'll have to play on excitement tonight*, I thought, *Johnny Gallo's "well-rested" suggestion is no longer an option.*

That evening was overcast and the darkness came early. The west wind was howling as we warmed up under the bright lights in the plush outfield grass of Dean Park. I noticed how big the Beaver Falls ballplayers looked compared to us. They were laughing and cocky and dismissing all the things we had accomplished.

"Did you hear that?" Harry whispered to me during infield practice. "They're saying we had a soft schedule. That we haven't faced anybody good until tonight."

"We *still* haven't faced anybody good," I shouted, loud enough for the Beaver Falls players to hear me. If they wanted a war of words, I wanted to make sure we didn't appear to be intimidated. But as I watched Tony warming up with

Beans near the home-team dugout I couldn't help but notice that he looked frail compared to the mighty Beaver Falls team.

With Tony on the mound, Dawson would play first base. But the rest of our infield looked tiny matched up to the Beaver Falls nine. And for the first time it caught my attention that while we wore the color-trimmed uniforms of the four-team Rockland Little League, the Beaver Falls players were wearing no fewer than a dozen different uniforms from their sixteen-team league.

In the top of the first, the rout began. The first two Beaver Falls batters lined base hits through our stunned infield. The ball seemed to explode off their bats. Then Harry booted an easy one-hopper to load the bases. It was his first error of the tournament. The pressure had beaten him for the moment, but Tony screamed, "Shake it off!" And Harry nodded that he was fine.

The wind was now whipping straight out to centerfield, and although Tony handcuffed their clean-up hitter with a sweet inside-corner curveball, the big left-hander fisted a fly ball toward DeLuca that caught a stiff breeze and sent Will all the way back to the warning track in center. The runners on second and third both tagged up and Beaver Falls had a 1–0 lead.

Their number-five hitter was a tough-looking kid named Roger Fontaine, who drove Tony's first pitch deep over the wall in left center. Just like that it was 4–0.

Coach Gallo knew we couldn't afford to get any further behind, and even though it was just the first inning, he jumped out of the dugout and pulled Tony in favor of the hard-throwing DeLuca.

Will walked the first batter he faced, but the next kid, another huge left-hander named Hal McGraw, smashed a shot to Tony at first, who turned the line drive into an inning-ending double play.

It was just the first inning, but we were already down 4–0. "It might be a long night," I whispered to Tony as we trotted off the field.

Beaver Falls started an eleven-year-old pitcher named Ronnie Rizzo. He was supposed to be their second-best pitcher, but he blew our first three hitters away on strikes. And before we could even catch our breath, we were back on defense.

When DeLuca started the second inning by walking the first two hitters, Johnny Gallo couldn't tolerate his wildness anymore and brought Harry in to pitch. It was deeper into our pitching staff than we had gone all season, and much further than we ever expected to go. With Harry on the mound, Coach Gallo actually brought Dawson in from centerfield and put him at shortstop.

I shook my head in disappointment. Dawson certainly had the arm to play the position, but a left-handed shortstop just made us look Bush League and second-class.

The first batter Harry faced was a kid named Kelly. He immediately hit a towering shot to left field that caught the howling wind and disappeared into the darkness so fast it may still be orbiting the earth. At least nobody on our team ever saw it land. It was 7–0 with no outs in the second inning.

After a high pop-out in the infield, Beaver Falls loaded the bases with two more singles and a walk. Finally, the next batter hit a hard grounder back to the mound that Harry speared and turned into a neat pitcher-to-catcher-to-first double play. Our defense had saved us for now, but with our number-four pitcher on the mound, and trailing 7–0 in the second inning, I could only imagine what the final score was going to be. It was our worst nightmare.

In the bottom of the second, Rizzo struck out our first two hitters (reaching five strikeouts in a row) before Ricky Baldwin finally drew a walk to give us our first base-runner. Now I stepped into the batter's box. Noticing my lack of size, their outfielders played very shallow, trying to cut off any bloop single I might drop in front of them.

But by this time the winds had grown incredibly strong, and when I lofted a routine fly ball to center, a gale-force wind grabbed it and drove it all the way to the warning track, where it fell safely to the ground. I pulled into second with a stand-up double, while Baldwin scampered home all the way from first.

We had closed to within 7–1, and the sight of their ten-year-old infielder standing at second base seemed to breathe some life back into the Rockland team members, who cheered wildly from the dugout.

And then I felt it. A huge drop of water whacked me in the eye. At first I thought one of the Beaver Falls players had spat at me, and then I got hit by another drop, then another. Soon I could hear heavy drops falling all around me. They sounded like machine-gun fire as they pelted the infield clay.

The storm hit so hard and so fast that Rizzo never threw another pitch. When I looked around, the umpires were waving us off the field, and I thought about the story my dad had told us the day before. "Just like that," he'd said, snapping his fingers, "the engines stopped." I couldn't help but wonder for an instant if God had had a hand in this.

As I retreated into the dugout I had mixed emotions. Sure, a rainout would give us a fresh start with Beaver Falls, but I just got my first extra-base hit of the tournament and drove in my first run. The rain would wipe those off the books. I would never admit to it out loud, but part of me hoped, just for an instant, that the skies would clear. Then just as quickly I forced the selfish thought from my head and joined my teammates in the dugout as they hooted and chanted for the rain to continue: to wash this nightmare away and give us a fresh shot at Beaver Falls.

Within ten minutes, the infield was a sea of mud and the rain showed no signs of letting up. The plate umpire walked out onto the saturated infield grass and waved his arms. The game would be postponed for two days. And since it was only the bottom of the second inning, we would start over from the beginning, 0–0.

"They're wiping away the runs," Tony smirked, as if he knew some inside joke.

"We get to start over with Dawson on the mound," I added with a knowing smile. And as we sat on the bench watching the water cascade off the first-base line and into the dugout, I again thought about my dad's war story: "A week later we were cruising back to the Philippines."

On the way back to the cars our coaches kept laughing and chanting a slogan I had never heard before: "Spahn and Sain and pray for rain." It was a reference to the 1948 Boston Braves, who had reached the World Series against the Cleveland Indians despite having only two high-quality starters, Warren Spahn and Johnny Sain.

The Braves went on to lose the series, but when game three was postponed by two days of rain, and game five was also postponed, Spahn and Sain ended up starting all six of the World Series games for the Braves. The Indians still won the series, four games to two.

It was the first time I had ever heard of that peculiar series, but I would never forget it again. "Baseball's a funny game," Tony reflected on the trip home. "I guess God's a Rockland fan."

I knew what my father would say if he were in the car: "God doesn't care who wins a baseball game." But I couldn't shake the feeling that fate had again played a part in our lives and, as usual, destiny had been on our side.

"I only have one question," Harry deadpanned. "Does that game count towards our earned run averages?"

"I have a different question," interjected Coach Slater, who was riding in the front seat next to Johnny Gallo. "Do you think the ball that Kelly hit off of you has landed yet?"

We all laughed, but deep down I wondered if even Dawson could stop this powerful Beaver Falls line-up.

chapter twenty-nine

Second Chances

"Are you kidding me?" Harry laughed as he sat down right next to me on the corner of his twin bed. "That's too good to be true. If you wrote a book like that, no one would ever believe it. I'll bet you were pissed about losing the double though."

"Truth is stranger than fiction," I offered. "But you know what's harder to believe? That you even know how unlikely that sudden rain was.

"They told me that you could barely remember your family. But here you are recognizing irony, understanding the pressures they put on us as kids, even realizing that I was disappointed about losing credit for a big hit. How do you explain that, Harry? How are we even having this conversation?"

"I'm not sure," he hesitated. "Sometimes I have good days. Sometimes I can see things; understand things. But usually, I'm lost. Even now, I don't remember Conti or Beans or DeLuca. I remember what you told me about them today, but I can't picture their faces or tell you anything else about them.

"I'm not even sure I'll remember *this* story, Teddy," he continued, looking away in shame.

"It doesn't matter if you remember the details," I answered. "All that matters is that you feel some pride. That you know who you are. That you don't think your whole life was just sitting around this gloomy room, wasting away.

"You're Harry fuckin' Kirkland!" I reminded him, jumping to my feet. "You were the starting shortstop on the most important baseball team in the history of that town. Every kid in Rockland wished that they were you.

"And it was 1964," I boasted. "Baseball was king in 1964. Nobody cared about the Steelers. Nobody cared about basketball or hockey. It was baseball. It was our battlefield, and you were right there in the middle of the battle."

"Finish the story, Teddy." He resolved, "I will remember it. I promise I will."

chapter thirty

The No-Hitter

The day after the rainout, we were back at practice. The dirt infield of the Rockland diamond was wet and sloppy, but Sammy Bellissimo's dad had picked up a truckload of sawdust somewhere, and all the coaches were shoveling it out over the puddles in the base paths. Sammy was the only eight-year-old on the team so he almost never got to play, but his family was just as involved as every other family in town when it came to supporting this team.

After a hot, humid, muddy day of practice, we all headed for DeVito's Drugstore to cool off with a Coke or soda. I don't think I was ever as dirty as I was that day.

I sat at the soda fountain, slurping down my second cherry Coke, when I heard the door swing open and a hush fall over the room. Suddenly, the crowd of filthy ballplayers parted like the Red Sea, and three gorgeous little girls made their way to the counter. It was Molly and Pam and Pam's cousin Becky. Molly was wearing a pale-blue blouse and white shorts. She had sunglasses on top of her head, holding back her soft brown hair. I had never seen her look as great as she did at that moment.

"Hi," I blurted, grinning from ear to ear.

"Hi, yourself," she smiled.

For a ten-year-old, I was pretty good at talking to girls, but with most girls, I could still act flustered and awkward and shy. Not with Molly; she made it easy for me. She just always knew the right thing to say.

"We're coming to the game tomorrow," she started. "My parents are going to take us."

I got up off my stool and offered it to her. Tony did the same with Pam.

Becky was Ray Marino's girlfriend, but he didn't get up. He seemed a little embarrassed that all his buddies were watching. He barely looked up from his Coke and all he said was, "How you doing?"

"That's great," I told Molly. "I'm glad you didn't come *last* night. We were lucky the rain blew in and washed out that nightmare." Tony shook his head. "We were lucky all right."

"Luck's got nothing to do with it," Molly answered. "I wrote my name in your hat. That's why it rained. As long as you wear my name in your hat, you can't lose."

Now Harry grabbed the baseball cap off my head and whistled. "She did write her name on it," he mocked, as he held up the inside brim for everyone to see. "Isn't that sweet?" And all my teammates laughed and started giving me the business.

Some of the comments were a little embarrassing, but I just kept staring at Molly's big brown eyes. When she locked in my gaze like that, I really didn't care what anyone said. I was crazy about that girl.

Molly pulled the cap out of Harry's hand and fitted it carefully back onto my head. Here I was, covered with mud from head to toe. My arms were crusty with sweat and sawdust, but my little angel was crowning me like a king.

"I'm sure that's why it rained," I teased. "I'm sure your autograph protected us."

"No use taking any chances," Tony chimed in. He grabbed a pen from behind the counter and handed it with his baseball cap to Pam.

She giggled as she wrote her name in big block letters on the underside of his brim. "Now you're protected too," she laughed.

"How about you, Ray?" taunted Terry Marino, putting his brother on the spot.

Becky reached for his ball cap, but Ray grabbed it first and shoved it under his butt on the soda fountain stool. "Forget it!" he shouted. "No girl's going to write on my hat. This is a baseball uniform, not a frickin' valentine."

Becky looked a little hurt as she ordered her lime soda. "Let Tony be the ladies' man," Ray explained to her. "I'm a man's man." And he looked at his brother for approval, but Terry just rolled his eyes. "We haven't heard the last of this," he told the counter-full of ballplayers, who all chuckled and shook their heads in agreement.

The next day, we were back at Dean Park for a seven-o'clock game. The New Castle Nationals had knocked off Ellwood City in the losers' bracket the night before. So the loser of our game would face the Nationals. The winner would sit back and wait to play for the tournament championship.

As we took infield practice, the Beaver Falls boys heckled us mercilessly. They knew we were shook up about the pounding we took in the rainout game. "Hey, short," shouted Kelly at Harry from the home-team dugout. "How come you're not pitching? I was hoping to launch a few more rockets tonight."

Our coaches had always told us to stay out of the trash-talking game, but Harry couldn't help himself. "You'll never hit Dawson," he spouted off to the big right-hander. "I can't wait to see you crawling back to the dugout with your tail between your legs!"

Derrick was warming up with Beans down the first-base side. "Kirkland, shut up!" he shouted at Harry. Dawson said very few words, but when he did everyone listened. "We'll do our talking on the field."

No one directed another word toward the Beaver Falls team; not then and not for the rest of the tournament.

But Dawson backed up every word that Harry had said. For the first three innings, he shut down the Beaver Falls lineup completely, with six strikeouts and no base runners.

Unfortunately, Beaver Falls had also rested their number-one pitcher, Roger Fontaine. And he tore through our undersized lineup with a blazing fastball, striking out seven and walking one in the first three innings.

It's funny now to think that Fontaine was their top pitcher, because Beaver Falls had two pitchers on their roster who would one day be drafted by Major-League teams: Ron Rizzo and Hal McGraw. They would become legendary American Legion and high school pitchers in Western Pennsylvania, but at this point in time, at the age of twelve, it was Fontaine who was the ace of the staff.

It was still 0–0 as Beaver Falls came to the plate in the bottom of the fourth. Dawson fanned the first two batters, but then Rizzo, who was playing second base and batting second, lined a shot over Harry's head at shortstop. It rolled all the way to the wall and Rizzo had the first hit of the game, a stand-up double.

Now with a runner on second and two outs, the next batter swung at the first pitch and sent a hard-spinning grounder off the end of the bat and directly to me at second. I charged hard and then got down on both knees to make sure the ball didn't get past me. It banged off my chest but rolled too far away for me to get the runner at first base.

It was tough to take. We had a chance to get out of the inning on that play and I booted it—my first error of the tournament. Rizzo had moved to third but couldn't score because the ball never left the infield. *At least I knocked it down*, I thought. But it was an error all the same.

I hung my head and Dawson hung his. It was just for a moment, but you rarely saw the big guy show any emotion. I remembered the game against Steve's Barbershop during the regular season when Dawson got angry at his shortstop for dropping the throw to second base, lost his concentration, and sent the next pitch right down the middle.

I called time-out and trotted toward the rubber to settle him down. "Sorry, Lefty," I said as I handed the ball back to him. Then I whispered, "You still got this, right?"

Now Ray and Harry and Tony joined us on the mound.

I hesitated for a second. "It's a left-hander," I said, looking in at the on-deck batter as my teammates entered the huddle. "That's a gift for you!"

We all looked in at the huge centerfielder as he entered the batter's box. It was their clean-up hitter, their star. A kid named DeMarco.

"Do *you* want to pitch to him?" said Dawson, a rare bit of wit from the kid who seldom spoke at all. We all cracked up… and the big southpaw smiled for a second. Then it was gone. "I'll get him," he nodded.

We all went back to our positions. Three curveballs later, we were trotting off the field. DeMarco never got his bat within five inches of a pitch. It was almost sad. I felt a little bit sorry for the kid. Everyone was depending on him. Everyone was expecting so much. But no twelve-year-old left-hander could hit Dawson's curve. And there probably weren't too many left-handed adults who could hit it either.

The game remained scoreless as we came to bat in the top of the fifth inning.

A muffled cheer went up from the Rockland fans and moans of anguish rolled from the Beaver Falls section of the bleachers. Yes, we had scored the first run of the game, but Ray was in obvious pain, so the Rockland faithful couldn't let out the delirious emotions they were feeling. Still, the buzz in the stands grew with every passing second.

Our entire coaching staff was on the field tending to Ray, and Tony, our on-deck hitter, moved in to pick up Ray's ball cap and wait for him to get to his feet. Ricky Baldwin had already touched home and I was just arriving at third base when I heard Tony laughing. He was trying to get my attention. I looked in toward home plate and saw him holding up the inside brim of Ray's hat. There was something written on it. *Becky*, it said.

Ray finally got to his feet and a huge ovation went up from crowd. There was nothing restrained about the cheering now. Ray was the town hero. He didn't back away. He took one for the team. "He fell on the live grenade," Jiggy would say later.

Tony hit a hard ground ball to shortstop to end the inning, but the damage had been done. If Dawson could hold these guys for two more innings, this almost impossible victory would be ours. It was still a tall order.

Incredibly, Dawson walked the first two batters in the bottom of the fifth. I was certain the next hitter would bunt, but instead he swung away and grounded a one-hopper toward the middle that Harry fielded, stepped on second and fired to first for a sweet double play. Then with the tying run at third, our big left-hander sent McGraw down on strikes and we had one more inning to go. "I guess they're too good to bunt," Harry smirked as we trotted off the field.

Fontaine had settled back into his rhythm, and we went one-two-three in the top of the sixth, but Beaver Falls was now down to their final at-bat.

Dawson got the first two hitters on strikes. But with two out, DeMarco, their clean-up hitter, rolled a ground ball between short and third for Beaver Falls' second hit of the game.

That brought Fontaine to the plate and he dug his cleats into the batter's box. We could all see this was going to be a war.

I took a quick look around the field at our defense. The Rockland uniforms were a sea of greens and blues, except for me and Tony and Harry. In our red hats and red-trimmed uniforms we stuck out like a sore thumb. There was no place to hide. For better or worse, it made everything we did seem magnified.

DeMarco took off for second, trying to steal, on the very first pitch. Beans' throw was in the dirt and I tried to short-hop it as the runner slid hard into my glove. For a moment, I thought we had him. I thought the game was over. But then I noticed, in agony, that the ball had come out of my glove and was rolling toward the outfield. If Harry hadn't been backing me up, DeMarco might have gone all the way to third.

The count on Fontaine was 0–1, and he battled with Dawson for the next seven pitches, fouling off two big breaking balls to run the count to 3–2. Finally Derrick reared back and fired a high strike and the batter lifted a long fly into deep right field.

Fontaine had already hit three home runs in the tournament, so Conti had been playing him fairly deep, but now he had his back up against the green wall. For the next five seconds, I felt sick to my stomach. A home run would beat us. After all the tense moments we had come through, after all the taunts and insults we had endured, we were still going to lose to these bastards. And it was my fault. I didn't hold the throw from Beans. We had one chance to beat them and now it was gone, just like this long fly ball.

The screams from the Beaver Falls' bench and fans were deafening. *Not good enough.* The thought echoed through my brain. *Not good enough.*

Then I saw Conti take a step forward. Then another step. Now he was in front of the warning track. Just like all our outfielders, he had been taught to find the fence first and then play the ball.

"Squeeze it, damn it," I mumbled to myself. "Squeeze it!" Billie put up both hands and calmly hauled in the long fly ball.

Tony and I were the first ones to reach Conti. And he leaped into our arms as the roar from the Rockland faithful reverberated across the finely groomed infield and echoed off the green outfield wall.

But Billie insisted on giving credit where credit was due and immediately only forty-five, that means I could be here for a long, long time. I thought it was almost over."

All the excitement and joy were gone from Harry's face now. And I marveled at how quickly this place, this hospital, could suck the life out of someone. I wondered how long I would last in a place like this, with its pale-green walls and steam radiators and rambling patients and condescending staff.

If only he could have stayed at home in Rockland, I thought. *If only he hadn't wised off to some stranger, then reached out and grabbed his wife's ass. Some luckless, brain-damaged soul makes one mistake and they send him to this hellhole. Is that really all it takes?*

We walked in silence down the long hallway and, as we stepped into the patient lounge, I noticed how desperately lonely the room seemed. One old woman sat trance-like in front of the TV, staring at a CNN report from somewhere in the Middle East, while an unshaven man in a dirty robe kept picking up the coffee pot and then placing it back on a hotplate without ever pouring any out. He mumbled to himself as he arranged and rearranged the Styrofoam cups on the counter into stacks of four, then eight, then back to four again. The rest of the room was empty and quiet.

"They treat me like a child here," Harry blurted out. "They count the forks and knives before and after dinner, and no one can leave the cafeteria until the count is right. And they have all kind of other stupid rules that don't make any sense. Look at that," he offered, pointing at a sign above the television.

"Do not touch TV," the poster barked in big block letters. "To change channels or volume, please see a staff member."

I could see that Harry's confidence was slipping away—that the excitement of the New Castle Little League Tournament was already starting to fade. I had to get him back somehow. I had to drag him back to the summer of 1964. If my story was going to make any lasting impression on Harry, I needed his undivided attention.

"There are a lot of rules that don't make sense," I cautioned him. "If they don't hurt you, who cares?

"Remember when we used to have those two-a-day practices in the searing heat, and the coaches told us not to drink water because it would make us sick?

Everybody knows that was bullshit now. But they would line us up at the water fountain next to the dugout and warn us not to swallow the water. We were supposed to just swish it around in our mouths and then spit it out."

"I do remember that," chuckled Harry. "I always swallowed some when they weren't looking." His mood was starting to improve.

"So did I, Harry," I laughed. "I'm sure we all did!"

"Do you remember when Tony's mother told us about green apples and ice cream?"

"Green apples and ice cream… What are you talking about?" He was grinning from ear to ear now.

"Sure," I said, "we had just finished eating that little basketful of green apples that your grandfather gave us. It was me, you, Tony, Stephanie, Connie, and Linda. Then we all walked down to the drugstore to get something to drink. The guys all ordered Cokes, but the three girls decided to share a banana split.

"My aunt Betty was helping out at the drugstore that day. She was manning the soda fountain, and when she overheard that we had just eaten those apples, she freaked out! She grabbed the banana split right out from under their noses and stuffed it down the sink. She said that mixing green apples and ice cream would *kill* us!"

"Get the hell out of here!" roared Harry. He was laughing so hard, his eyes began to tear up.

"She was serious," I continued. "She swore that some little kid they grew up with had eaten green apples and ice cream and then threw up until his insides came out."

"You're bullshitting me," Harry sputtered, grabbing his sides as he shook with laughter.

"They had us convinced too," I said. "Stephanie had already eaten a spoonful of the ice cream. She was sure she was going to die. She cried for hours."

"Where would Betty get an idea like that?" Harry shook his head as he wiped away a tear.

"My mother swore it was true, too," I told him. "They both believe it to this day."

"But why?"

"Who knows," I answered. "Maybe some little kid got sick and died from the flu or TB, and that was the story their parents told them so they could make some kind of sense out of a senseless tragedy. Anyway, I never questioned it. Why should I? It was no big sacrifice to avoid eating green apples with my ice cream. It was a stupid rule, sure. But it didn't really hurt anybody.

"Just like opening your mouth and sticking out your tongue after taking your meds doesn't really hurt you. Sometimes you just have to roll with it even if it seems ridiculous."

"Teddy," Harry offered after a minute or two, "I want to hear the rest of the baseball story now. I want to know if Dick could beat those guys again."

"Who?" I hesitated. "Oh, you mean *Derrick*, Derrick Dawson?" His statement confused me for a second. Dawson was a Rockland legend. No one who grew up there would ever call him *Dick*. It would be like an American schoolchild calling the father of our country *Greg* Washington. It made me feel a little uneasy, but I shook it off and dove back into my account of the tournament.

"Dawson's second battle against Beaver Falls was the greatest game I can ever remember," I told him with an appreciative nod. "It was an epic struggle."

chapter thirty-two

The War

Johnny Gallo called for a light workout on the morning of our next showdown with Beaver Falls. It was a Monday and the game was scheduled for 7 p.m. We were getting together around ten o'clock for batting practice and a couple rounds of infield. As expected, Beaver Falls had battered the New Castle Nationals, this time 13–5.

"New Castle scored two runs on Rizzo, then three more on Kelly," Cam Slater, one of our assistant coaches, told us at practice that Monday morning. "They had some big hitters, but Beaver Falls just kept pounding the ball."

Cam's younger cousin, Jerry Slater, played for Beaver Falls and Cam had scouted the game for us on Saturday night. "Jerry had two big hits," our coach recounted, "but they told him he was *sitting* for tonight's game."

"They're benching Jerry Slater?" Tony blurted out. "How is that possible?"

We had all read stories in the local newspaper about Jerry's heroics in the Beaver Falls Little League. He could really hit a baseball and was a slick fielder with a good arm. He would have been one of our best players if he lived in Rockland. But the Beaver Falls all-star team had so much talent that Jerry Slater started only half their games.

"They might have better players, but we have a better team," Harry rationalized, as we stood together near second base between rounds of infield. "I mean, we know each other better."

He was right, of course. We had practiced together twice a day every day since July first: over *sixty* practice dates. The Beaver Falls all-star team only had *four* practices as a team all year. Sure, they practiced with their regular city league teams until the end of July, but they didn't even pick their all-star team until their regular season ended. So they hadn't really played together the way we had.

"That's our biggest advantage," I said and nodded back to him. "We always know who the cutoff man is and where he's going to be. We know who's covering first on a bunt and who's backing up second on a steal."

"They *do* hit the shit out of the ball, though." Harry's voice trailed off as he returned to his position at shortstop and waited for the next ground ball.

I chuckled nervously as I watched him walk away. Beaver Falls had scored in double digits in every one of their five tournament victories. *How long can Dawson shut these guys out?* I wondered.

The Beaver Falls newspaper, the *News Tribune*, covered the action of every Beaver Falls Little League game all season long. Most families in Rockland subscribed to the *Tribune* so we already knew a lot about their players. Their names had been in the headlines for months. They were like celebrities to us.

Ellwood City and New Castle also had their own daily newspapers, and they carried a lot of local sports coverage too. It always made their players seem bigger than life. It made the task of stopping them seem to be just that much tougher.

Of course, Derrick Dawson is also bigger than life. I comforted myself with the thought as I waited for the next ground ball. *And now the biggest game of his life is just a few hours away.*

Coach Gallo gathered us together in the dugout at the end of practice. "You know the New Castle tournament is double elimination," he reminded us. "That means Beaver Falls has to beat us twice, while we only have to beat them one more time. But Derrick is rested now, so we're throwing him tonight. If we lose, we play tomorrow night. But we're *not* going to lose."

Johnny Gallo wasn't bragging. He was telling us something we already knew: we would be putting everything we had into this game; we weren't saving anything for tomorrow. If they beat Dawson, we would have to come back with one of our lesser pitchers, and we couldn't have that. We needed to win tonight.

"They're going to throw Fontaine again tonight," the coach continued. "If he gets wild, we'll probably *take* a strike… or even two. So keep your eyes on me for the signal."

"Now go home and rest. No swimming, no Whiffle Ball, no big meals. We'll meet back here at five o'clock."

But going home and resting was the furthest thing from our minds. We were too excited to rest. After practice, Tony, Harry, and I hopped on our bikes and headed for the drugstore. We got to the door just as my Uncle Raymond, Connie's dad, was about to enter. He held the door for us and then bellowed, "Get these boys whatever they want, Jiggy. Their money's no good in here today."

I sat down at the counter and ordered a cherry Coke. Tony had a regular Coke, while Harry, taking advantage of Uncle Ray's offer, ordered a big chocolate milkshake. "Drink that slowly," cautioned Jiggy. "You don't want an upset stomach for the game tonight."

Every person who entered the pharmacy for the next half hour tried to buy us something. I ended up eating a Snickers bar, a bag of potato chips and a blue Popsicle. It was like we were soldiers shipping out to war, and everyone who saw us wanted to buy us a drink. We sat there beaming as we stuffed down all the junk food we could eat.

Then we hopped back on our bikes and headed uptown, our baseball gloves flapping on our handlebars. The warm August air blew across our faces as we waved or shouted out a greeting to everyone we rode past. I loved that one-speed bike, red and swift and solidly built. It was my mobility and freedom. On my bicycle, I could be anywhere in Rockland in less than five minutes—and everything I ever wanted was in Rockland.

When we got to Popovic's supermarket on Third Avenue, there was a bevy of young girls on the sidewalk surrounding Will DeLuca, Billie Conti, and Ricky Baldwin. Pam and Molly were among them and, as we drove up, I could see that one of the girls, Janet Slater, was signing her name on the inside brim of Will's baseball hat.

"I see you started quite a trend," I laughed to Molly as I threw down my kickstand and hopped off my bike. She ran straight toward me and for a second I thought she was going to wrap her arms around me. But she stopped at the last second and stood just inches away, smiling and glowing… pretty as a rose.

"Will and Janet are going together," she beamed.

I looked more than a little surprised. "I didn't even know they *knew* each other."

"They do now," Molly giggled. And DeLuca held up his hat with Janet's name written on it.

Billie did him one better: his hat had no fewer than four different girls' names inscribed inside the brim—Sherry, Ginny, Linda, and Connie. "They can't *all* be your girlfriends," I chuckled.

"Why not?" answered Conti. And everybody cracked up.

Then a girl from Second Avenue named Alice Landers grabbed Harry's hat off his head. She already had her pen in hand. "Can I sign it?" she cooed at him. "Uh, sure," Harry replied.

Despite his curly black hair and his boyish freckles and good looks, Harry was a little bashful, and I'm certain he barely knew this girl. "So is she your girlfriend now?" I taunted.

"I don't know," he answered. "She's cute though, isn't she?"

"They're *all* cute," I told him. And I was right. Rockland was filled with gorgeous little girls.

That's how the rest of the afternoon went. Every person on the street wanted to chat. Every car that drove by honked its horn, every driver flashed us the "thumbs up" sign. Some of the veterans in town shot us the V-for-victory sign instead.

Just two or three years later, that gesture came to symbolize the peace movement, a symbol of defiance and antigovernment rebellion. But in 1964 it didn't mean *peace*, it meant only *victory*.

It was the best afternoon of my life, but as three o'clock became three-thirty, the mood turned somber and reflective. I coasted my bike back down Fourth Avenue toward home. The streets had grown quiet as a painting, and the white plumes of smoke looked like manmade clouds as they rose out of the B & W plant and filled the eastern sky. The town of Rockland was simmering in the hot summer sun. I hopped off my bike and ran inside the house.

As I pulled on my red-trimmed uniform that afternoon, I wondered if we could possibly beat these guys again. I looked at the front of my game shirt. "Board of Trade," it blasted across the front in red script lettering. I shook my head and sighed. The truth was, the Rockland Board of Trade didn't really exist anymore. It hadn't existed since the stone quarry had closed down twenty years earlier.

The town once had movie theaters, department stores, and its own train station, but Rockland had only six businesses in town now. Uncle Joe called his team "Board of Trade" because when Babcock and Wilcox opened its steel mill in Rockland, he envisioned a return to prosperity and a lively retail market. And although the town did recover substantially from the Depression, it never quite became as prosperous as people had hoped.

And now I was going into battle with that symbol of lost prosperity splashed across my chest. *If this Beaver Falls team beats us by twenty runs—and they're certainly capable of doing it—the whole town will be deflated, not just the ballplayers,* I thought.

Dawson was the key, of course. If he could shut them out again, we had a great chance. But what if *we* got shut out by Fontaine? We hadn't *really* scored on him in the first game. The kid got shook up and walked three batters, and then hit Ray in the back. That's not exactly a *rally.*

We have to hit him this time, I resolved.

In the *best*-case scenario, Dawson could only shut them out for six innings. After that we'd have to bring in Tony or Will. No—we had to score in the first six innings or we'd get beat, and maybe in humiliating fashion.

Johnny Gallo and Uncle Joe had said that our strategy going in was to play solid defense and find a way to scrape out a run or two. I was nervous, but my job was really even simpler than that. *Try as hard as you can to do exactly what the coaches tell you to do,* I chided myself like a soldier in basic training.

Sometimes it's better not to worry about what you're doing. Sometimes it's just better to do what you're told. I found that thought comforting somehow, and I shrugged off my anxiety and replaced it with the excitement of a ten-year-old who's about to play in the biggest game of his life.

Just as I finished buttoning up my uniform, my brother Nelson walked into our room. "What time's the game start?" he asked.

"Seven o'clock," I told him. "Are you going?'

"The whole town's going to be there," he shrugged. "I might as well go."

Nelson wasn't good at expressing his feelings, but I knew he was happy for me. The best Little-League players in the county were going to be on that field tonight, and I'd be the only ten-year-old out there. It was a dream come true, but Nelson wasn't one to throw compliments around. So he stood in silence as I pulled on my red baseball cap and rounded off the visor.

"Keep your eyes on my girlfriend for me," I asked as I pulled my cleats from the closet. "Make sure none of those Beaver Falls kids are flirting with her."

"If anyone talks to her I'll kick their ass for you." Nelson was beaming now. This was a show of affection he could understand. "I don't care how big they are."

"I know she'll be in good hands," I answered. And I slapped him on the shoulder as I made my way down the stairs.

We arrived at Dean Park about an hour before game time. There was no trash-talking this time, just focus. Both teams took solid ten-minute rounds of infield, and the ball whipped around the bases and cracked into fielders' gloves while the incessant chatter from the coaches and players filled the stadium with energy.

I didn't see an error or even a bobbled ball from either team during the entire workout. It reminded me of the old war newsreels showing the troops marching before a reviewing stand. Every move was sharp and crisp.

Twenty-eight teams had started this tournament, and now it was down to two. I didn't know if we were really one of the two best teams in the tournament, but I was sure of one thing—we were the best-*trained* team.

Harry seemed to read my mind. "That's what a thousand rounds of infield will do for you," he grinned as we trotted off the field and headed to the dugout.

When we got inside, Coach Gallo was shaking his head as if he were cursed. "We're visitors again, boys," he chuckled, and a collective groan went up from all the ballplayers. The umpires flipped a coin before every game to determine home team and, except for the Bessemer game, we had lost every flip.

"That's OK," barked Jiggy. "We get first crack at 'em."

"Don't worry," added Tony, slapping me on the back, "We've been visitors every game and we've won every game. We wouldn't want to change our streak now."

As soon as we found our seats on the bench, a hush fell over the entire team. Coach Gallo now stood before us, unblinking, determined. He had been our unquestioned leader for the entire season. No one ever answered him back. No one ever ignored his bunt signals or argued about the batting order. We had complete faith in him. His word was law. But now, as we sat facing him before the biggest game of our lives, all he said was, "Jiggy has something to say to you boys."

Uncle Joe rose slowly and began pacing back and forth, up and down the bench. His dream was at hand, and he weighed every word he was going to say carefully. As he passed, he looked each one of us directly in the eye.

"Some people say you don't belong here," he started. "They say you're too small... that you don't have the talent of these city teams. But it takes more than talent to be a winner. It takes hard work and determination and guts.

"I hear their comments out there. They're calling us lucky. They're saying we're a one-man team. Well, let me tell you something right now: there's no such thing as a one-man team!

"And talent?" he growled. "The world is full of talented losers!

"I don't know if you're the best team in the tournament or not. But I know one thing: no one has worked harder than you have.

"Sure, Beaver Falls has 25,000 residents... New Castle has 40,000... Rockland has about 900. So maybe they're right. Maybe you are lucky. Maybe you don't belong here. But you're here now, and if you win one more game, then you're the champions. Now that's something they can never take away from you. You'll carry the memory of this game with you for the rest of your lives.

"But remember," he commanded, "you're not just playing this game for yourselves. You're playing for your friends and family. You're playing for your town. Just make sure you play hard and do your best. That's all we can ask of you, and all you can ask of yourselves."

There was a buzz of excitement in the dugout as Ray Marino picked up his bat and helmet and headed for the batter's box. Then a roar from the Beaver Falls fans as their team took the field. "Come on, Ray," Tony coaxed as he took his place on the on-deck circle. "Get us started."

I felt sure that tonight we would jump on the Beaver Falls ace right away, but this game began just like the first game. It was another pitchers' duel. Our first five batters went down on strikes. Finally, with two out in the top of the second inning, big Ricky Baldwin lined a 2–0 pitch up the middle for our first base hit, and although I followed with a weak ground ball to second base to close out the inning, our hitless streak had ended, and Fontaine's air of invincibility had ended with it.

Meanwhile, Dawson looked even stronger than he had in the first game (if that's possible). He struck out seven of the first nine batters he faced, and at the end of four innings, he hadn't allowed even one base-runner. Those Beaver Falls batters who managed to hit the ball at all had grounded weakly to the right side. Tony and I had each handled two ground balls without an error.

When we came to bat in the top of the fifth inning, there was a growing concern that our team was in real trouble. Little-League games are only six innings long, and tournament rules said no pitcher was allowed to throw more than six innings in any three-day period. If Fontaine and Dawson both continued to throw shutout ball for two more innings, both starters would have to be pulled from the game.

Beaver Falls was loaded with top-notch pitchers, so their drop-off in talent would be minimal. But the drop-off from Dawson to Tony or Will DeLuca was huge. We needed to score right now and we all knew it.

Dawson, our number-five hitter, stepped into the batter's box to lead off the fifth inning. On Fontaine's first pitch, the tall left-handed swinger lined a double off the wall in left-center field. The stadium was shaking with the sound of half-crazed Rockland fans. The roar was so loud I couldn't hear myself think. Finally, Uncle Joe's voice broke through the din. "Teddy, you're on deck."

Ricky Baldwin was stepping to the plate, and as I made my way to the on-deck circle I felt like the eyes of the entire ballpark were on me. I took a quick look into the stands and saw the faces of my mother and father, my grandparents, my brother, my little sister Sophie, Molly and Pam, and all the neighborhood kids. It seemed that everyone I ever knew was watching.

I could see that Fontaine was shaken up. His first fastball to Baldwin bounced in the dirt for a wild pitch, and Dawson moved over to third. Now we had no outs and the leading run just sixty feet away. Beaver Falls pulled their infielders up on the base paths. Any hard-hit ground ball would now have a good chance of getting through the drawn-in infield.

I closed my eyes and said a quick prayer that Ricky would get another hit; that he would bounce one up the middle or even hit a sacrifice fly; anything to get us the lead and take the pressure off me. But the Beaver Falls hurler was starting to lose his concentration, and Baldwin eventually walked on a 3–2 pitch. That brought the Beaver Falls coach out to the mound to try and calm down his ace.

We had the bottom of our batting order coming to the plate: me… then Conti… then Harry; three chances to score right now. But during the time-out, Coach Gallo called me down to the third base coaches' box. "We need you to take a strike," he ordered, "and if this guy gets behind in the count, we might need you to take *two* strikes."

I didn't know what to say. I had a chance to win this game with one swing, but Fontaine was too good to give up the plate for two strikes. That would only leave me one pitch to hit. I dropped my head in silence.

"I know you want to hit," said the coach. "But this kid's falling apart. You remember what happened last game… He *forced* in the winning run. This is our best chance."

I appreciated the explanation, but it really wasn't necessary. He knew I'd do whatever he ordered me to do. That's how we got this far in the first place: by doing exactly as we were told.

As I stepped into the batters' box, I could hear Jiggy's mantra for the proper way to "take" a pitch: "No one should know you're taking the pitch," he had instructed us. "If the umpire knows you're not going to swing, he's more likely to call it a strike. Just stand in there and follow the pitch all the way into the catcher's glove."

Fontaine's first pitch was in the dirt and, although the catcher blocked it, it rolled about six feet away from him. Ricky Baldwin slid safely into second with Dawson still holding at third.

Now we had second and third and nobody out. Johnny was right about one thing: Fontaine was struggling. But his next pitch came right down the middle and I dutifully watched it go by for strike one.

I stepped out and checked the coach's signal at third. No "take" sign now; I was swinging away. But when the Beaver Falls ace missed the outside corner with his next two pitches, I was looking at a 3–1 count.

For a moment I thought about not looking at Johnny Gallo for a signal. If I never stepped out and looked at the coach, then he couldn't blame me for swinging away. Three-and-one is a hitter's count. I knew he had to split the plate with the next pitch. It was my best chance to beat him. But of course I *did* step out and look. And of course Coach Gallo was flashing me the "take" sign again.

I followed the next pitch from the time it left the pitcher's hand until the time it struck the catcher's mitt. "Strike two," the umpire barked. And I could hear a gasp of despair from the Rockland faithful.

It's not fair, I thought. *No one in the ballpark even knows I had to take that pitch. They just figure I'm a ten-year-old punk who's overmatched.*

"Come on, Teddy," I could hear Coach Gallo encouraging me now. "Get a good swing on it. Just put it in play."

The pitch was a chest-high fastball and I swung as hard as I could but came up empty. "Strike three!" screamed the ump as the Beaver Falls fans roared their approval.

I slunk back toward the dugout. All I had had to do was hit the ball hard somewhere, anywhere. But instead, I struck out. I couldn't bear to look into the stands and all those disappointed faces. When I got back to the bench, no one said a word.

Conti stepped into the batter's box and chased a curveball off the outside corner for strike one.

"Were you taking?" Tony whispered as I sat down next to him on the bench.

I nodded.

"How many strikes?"

"Two," I answered.

"Jesus!" he said. "How can they put the handcuffs on you like that?"

I just bowed my head in disappointment.

"Don't worry, cousin," he told me. "Conti will get him home."

But as he said it, Fontaine hit the outside corner for the second strike. "Come on, Billie," I pleaded. "Put it in play, baby."

The crowd was still buzzing at a fever pitch. The pressure on Conti was incredible. The next pitch was high, but Billie was already swinging. "Strike three," howled the umpire. And the Beaver Falls fans roared again. Inside our dugout, a collective groan went up from the entire team.

Harry moved into the batter's box now as their infielders backed up to their normal positions. With two outs there could be no "seeing-eye" ground ball slipping through the drawn-in infield, no sacrifice fly driving in the run from third. Only a real base hit could save us now, and Harry was our number-nine hitter.

Everyone in our dugout rose to their feet and peered through the green protective screen in front of us. Dawson stood motionless at third base, hands on his hips, no expression on his face. Ricky Baldwin fidgeted at second, looking nervously at Coach Gallo for any possible signal he might be flashing to the batter or the runners. But the time for signals and strategy was over. It was man-on-man now, and only Roger Fontaine and Harry Kirkland could resolve the matter.

The right-handed ace reached back and fired an outside-corner fastball. "Strike one," the umpire barked, and we all dropped our heads in dismay.

The crowd, which had been alternately thunderous then still, rumbled continuously now—a constant, escalating roar. Harry pulled down on his batting helmet, bobbed his head a few times to shake off the pressure, and stepped back into the batter's box.

Fontaine reached back and fired again, another outside-corner fastball. Harry took a good swing, a short, compact stroke, but couldn't quite reach the pitch. "Strike two," howled the ump. But I could barely hear his voice over the roar of the Beaver Falls fans. Fontaine had now thrown seven straight strikes.

"Grab your rags," moaned Tony in disgust as he picked up his first-baseman's mitt and slammed it against the wall of the dugout. A puff of dust floated into the air and I waved it away to clear my view.

Uncle Joe, who had been kneeling near the steps of the dugout, fiercely turned to face his son and for a second I thought he was going to rip Tony's head off. But there would be time for that later. For now, his attention—everyone's attention—was fixed on Harry.

I looked into the stands behind home plate. No one was sitting. Everyone was on their feet—everyone except Harry's mom, who had her face buried in her hands. His father, who had once parachuted into German machine-gun fire, had a clenched fist pressed against his lips.

The bright lights of Dean Park bathed the entire scene in a harsh glow against the black, moonless sky, and every face, every detail seemed crystal-clear and completely in focus.

Harry took a few quick practice swings, stretched his shoulders and neck, and stepped back into the batter's box, crowding the plate as best he could.

"Throw your hands," barked Jiggy from the dugout. "Trust your swing."

I could see the catcher setting up for an outside pitch as Fontaine went into his windup. Harry stood motionless at the plate. I remember thinking that the Beaver Falls ace was throwing as hard as Dawson, but without the pinpoint control.

Last game we beat him on a bad pitch, I thought. *But this time, the pitch needs to be good... too good.*

Fontaine reached back and fired. He wanted to hit the outside corner, but instead his fastball came right down the middle and Harry swung: a split-second late, but right on the ball. He hit a slicing line drive, just over the outstretched hands of the leaping first baseman.

"Stay fair," I screamed. "Stay fair."

The ball landed inches inside the right field line, then bounded into the corner as a deafening roar filled the stadium. Dawson scored easily, with Baldwin hot on his heels.

Harry hit first base and then streaked toward second. The cheers rolled like thunder across the field, making it impossible for him to hear Coach Gallo's instructions. "Stay up… Stay up," the coach screamed, but his voice was lost in the din. And although there was no play at second, Harry dove head-first into the bag.

Inside the dugout, we bounced and hugged and howled at the top of our lungs. In the crowd it was pandemonium. Women were crying. Men were embracing. Young girls were dancing on their seats.

We all ran from the dugout to greet Dawson and Baldwin as Harry lay out on the infield dirt, still hugging the second-base bag. The cheering refused to abate, but it gradually changed from a roar to a chant. "Harry… Harry… Harry," the crowd reverberated.

The little shortstop slowly rose to his feet, grinning from ear to ear. His eyes were wide open and danced back and forth from the fans to the coaches to the euphoric team. He was taking it all in, absorbing every sight and sound. So that he would never forget it.

"He did it," laughed Tony. "The son of a bitch did it!"

"And *you're* lucky he did," added Uncle Joe. Although it was obvious that Tony's momentary lapse of faith was no longer an issue now.

I don't remember how the inning ended or when the cheering finally stopped, but when we returned to the field for the bottom of the fifth, there was still electricity in the air. We could almost taste victory.

Dawson had not allowed even one base-runner to this point, but with two outs in the fifth, he issued his first base-on-balls, spoiling his bid for a perfect game. Two pitches later, Boller, the Beaver Falls shortstop, lined a base hit up the middle, and a hush fell over the crowd.

Dawson's very next pitch was in the dirt, and Beans dropped to his knees to smother the ball, then spun around and around trying to locate it. The runners took off.

"In your glove, Beans," I screamed from second base. The ball had somehow gotten wedged in the webbing of his mitt, but by the time he realized it, Beaver Falls had runners at second and third.

The Beaver Falls fans were screaming wildly now. A base hit could tie the game. Immediately their bench came to life, but not with cheers, not with hopefulness. Instead they heaped ridicule on the Rockland catcher and then on our whole team. Beans tried to laugh it off with a dismissive shrug, but the jeers continued.

"A bunch of punks," one player screamed from the dugout. "Bush League," chided another. "Just put it in play," taunted Boller from second base. "They won't field it."

I felt the anger welling up inside me. These bastards were still trying to shake us, trying to intimidate us, trying to bully us into submission. I looked over at Tony at first base and Harry at short, both pacing around like caged lions in their red-trimmed Board of Trade uniforms. I dug my cleats into the infield clay and crouched down into my set position.

McGraw, one of their tall left-hand hitters, was at the plate. Dawson had already struck him out on a big breaking pitch in the third inning, but this time Derrick's first pitch hung up in the strike zone and McGraw smashed a hard ground ball toward the hole between first and second. I took two quick steps then dove as far as I could toward the ball. I had to knock it down somehow. If it got through to the outfield, the game would be tied. I had to get some part of me in front of that ball.

Then I felt it smack into my glove. I bounced up to my knees, pulled the ball from the webbing and fired to Tony at first. McGraw was out by two steps. "A tremendous play by the second-baseman," squawked the public address announcer into the black August sky. And the celebration started all over again.

I flew off the field, jumping and bounding like an antelope on a *National Geographic* special. When I reached the dugout, I leaped into Johnny Gallo's arms and he hoisted me over his head like the Stanley Cup.

The Rockland faithful were delirious, while the Beaver Falls fans, their coaches, and most of all their players were done, beaten, comatose.

As I walked toward the water fountain between innings, I was floating on the sea of pride emanating from the Rockland faithful. One of the Beaver Falls coaches caught sight of me. He was talking to someone in the stands behind home plate. "We just can't score on Dawson and that damn red infield," he cursed.

On the way back to the dugout I passed our big left-hander kneeling in the on-deck circle. He had a blue jacket draped over his left arm, while the right sleeve hung to the ground behind him. "Hey, Dawson," shouted a particularly bitter Beaver Falls fan from behind the screen. "You ought to move to BF next year. Imagine what you could do with *that* team behind you."

Derrick looked out at the talented Beaver Falls lineup with its stacked roster of power hitters and prima donnas at every position. "That's not a team," he said dryly, shrugging. Then he nodded toward the Rockland dugout. "This is a team."

We didn't score in the top of the sixth, but nobody seemed to mind.

And in the bottom of the inning, Beaver Falls went down without even a whimper. Dawson struck out the side to end the game, setting off the biggest celebration in Rockland since V-J Day.

chapter thirty-three

A Glimpse of Heaven

Harry was jumping around the patient lounge now. He high-fived the lady who was silently staring at the television. "We won!" He grabbed her by the shoulders. "We beat Beaver Falls."

"They're talking about you!" pleaded the old woman, pointing at the CNN reporter on the screen. "They know you're here. They're saying terrible things about you."

The old woman's delusions surprised me, but not Harry. He rolled with her comments and kept bouncing and laughing. "Who cares?" he told her. "They can't hurt me. Nobody can hurt me. Know why? 'Cause we're the champs! That's why!"

He bounded across the room toward the patient who had once again picked up the coffee pot and was about to replace it on the hotplate. "Here, let me get that for you," Harry laughed, pouring out a cup of coffee into one of the Styrofoam cups. "Drinks are on me!"

The disheveled man in the dirty robe just looked down at the cup in his hand. "Oh... no... no," he moaned. And with his free hand he immediately restacked the remaining cups in groups of four, then held the full cup of coffee at arm's length, like Superman scrutinizing a lump of kryptonite.

I just sat there laughing as Harry leaped and bounced around the room. "We beat them, Teddy. We beat that unbeatable team."

"And you're the reason, Harry. You drove in both our runs. I couldn't do it. I choked. So did Conti. But you saved us. You came through. You made heroes of us all."

Just then big James, who had been following us at a distance, came through the door to the patient lounge. "What's going on in here?" His grouchiness had been replaced by a big smile. "What's the celebration?"

"We won, James," Harry blurted, "and I got the double to win the game."

"Where?" he wondered, looking around the lounge for some explanation. "When?"

"Dean Park," I chuckled, "1964."

Harry was again hopping around James like a sparring partner, throwing punches into the air.

"1964," moaned his roommate. "That's ancient history."

"Not to Harry it's not; to him it just happened." I put my hands on both their shoulders. "You're rooming with a star here. The hero of the Rockland Little League All-Stars."

"What's all the noise in here?" came a woman's voice from the doorway. It was the pastel nurse with a clipboard in her hands.

"Just telling some old baseball stories," I smiled. "Just remembering a huge game that Harry won for us."

"Do *you* remember that game, Mr. Kirkland?" She seemed concerned. "Can you picture it?"

"I can picture it now," he laughed. "I can hear the people cheering. I can see my mother crying and my dad with his hands raised over his head, and everyone pouring out on the field. I can picture it all."

"But do you really *remember* it?" she probed. "Or are you visualizing the story your friend just told you?" Harry looked a little frustrated.

"What difference does it make?" I offered. "He's living it right now. He's a champion *right now*. He'll never forget that."

"OK, Champ." She smiled and nodded her head. "But it's 4:30, time for dinner. Please line up at the elevator."

"I have to hear about the celebration," Harry whined. "I have to find out if the town was excited; if the people were happy; if we had a parade. Can't I skip a meal?"

"Dinner is over at 5 o'clock," she announced with that flat smile pasted to her face. "Your guest can wait here until you return if he'd like."

My one-hour visit was now five hours long. "Sure, I'll wait," I said after a long pause. "I can't leave without finishing the story."

Yes! Harry laughed. "I'll eat fast, you'll see. I'll be back before you know it." He put his arm on James' shoulder and bounded out of the room, followed by the pastel nurse and troop of patients who waddled after her like baby ducklings.

I looked down at the frame in my hands and studied all the smiling young faces again. *What a night that was*, I thought. *Maybe the best night ever.*

chapter thirty-four

Joy on the Home Front

There were at least thirty cars in the caravan that rolled back into Rockland that Monday night. We were joined by about twenty more cars that were parked along Route 18 just outside of town.

As we turned down Main Street, we saw two police cars and a fire engine parked along the side of the road, sirens howling and lights flashing. "What happened here?" Tony chirped from the back seat, looking for the accident or fire that might have caused the disturbance.

"They're here for you," laughed Coach Gallo from the front seat as the first police car pulled out in front of us, followed by the fire truck. "They're leading the procession."

We all hung out the windows, waving our trophies in the air and shouting to the people who were lining the streets. Although it was after 10 p.m., it seemed that everyone in town who wasn't in the convoy was standing along the road to greet us as we drove through Rockland. Horns were blasting, sirens were howling, red and blue lights were flashing, and ballplayers were screaming and waving our hats and hands at everyone we saw.

"We won!" Harry howled into the black sky.

"We're the champs!" Tony shouted out the back window. "We knocked off Beaver Falls."

"Twice," I screamed, as I tried to force my head out the same window. And everyone in the car hooted and cheered. It was mass hysteria.

After weaving our way through town for fifteen minutes, the caravan, with horns still blaring, began to arrive at the Italian Club on Second Avenue. I didn't think there could be anyone left in Rockland, but a huge crowd had gathered outside the club.

As the players got out of the cars, Timmy Bianchi, one of our assistant coaches, barked out our names over a police megaphone and the crowd cheered wildly. Every ballplayer, both starters and reserves, was applauded as he made his way down the sidewalk. Tony and I both got tremendous ovations—after all we were related to half the town. Molly and Pam were in the throng, and so were Stephanie, Connie, and Linda, and everyone was laughing and smiling and hugging each other.

When Harry was introduced, the crowd went crazy, and began chanting his name again: "Harry… Harry… Harry." He was beaming.

"What a moment for Harry," Tony sighed. "He must be the happiest kid in the world."

Of course, the loudest and longest ovation was saved for Derrick Dawson. It was absolute pandemonium when he stepped out of the final vehicle. And all the players rushed up, hoisted him on our shoulders and carried him into the Italian Club, bouncing him through the crowd as we went.

The team made its way to the front stage in the banquet room as the building quickly filled to capacity. Finally Johnny Gallo grabbed the microphone and addressed the rowdy townspeople.

"We had 'em all the way!" barked Coach Gallo, stealing one of Pirates radio announcer Bob Prince's signature phrases. And the crowd roared its approval again.

"You'll never know how hard these boys worked to bring this back to you," he announced, holding the championship trophy over his head. "Every day, twice a day, they were down at that ball field in the dust and the heat. They didn't go swimming like other kids. They didn't go to amusement parks. They didn't go on vacations. They dedicated themselves to this team and to this town.

"They spent hundreds of hours this summer working on batting and bunting and sliding and running the bases. They took over a thousand rounds of infield and outfield practice. Then they went out and battled with the best teams in Western Pennsylvania and conquered them all, including mighty Beaver Falls, who they beat not once, but twice."

The cheers rose again and the noise was deafening. Tony was standing beside me and tried to shout over the din, but it was no use. I couldn't hear a word he was saying. The coach finally raised his hand to ask for quiet.

"I want to thank you for all your support this year," he offered. "This turnout is tremendous, but not surprising. We always knew you were behind us. We could see it when you came out to watch us practice. We could feel it as we walked down the streets of this town. Simply put, there are no better fans on earth than Rockland fans."

The ovation from the standing-room-only crowd shook the building. Johnny Gallo was still talking, but no one could hear him. We just watched as he passed the microphone over to Jiggy.

A huge smile lit up Uncle Joe's face as he waited for the cheering to subside, but his eyes were puffy and red. "When we started this league eight years ago," he began, "we tried to give our kids the chance to be their best. Some had been going to Ellwood City or Beaver Falls or New Galilee for a chance to play ball, but we knew they weren't getting a fair shake. So we started our own league and we scraped and scratched to find ballplayers. We recruited boys who had never played ball a day in their life. We had kids five and six years old out on the field competing with twelve-year-olds, just to get enough players to fill our rosters.

"It was the dedication of the coaches—and not just the coaches you see on this stage tonight but all the men out there who have given their time to our boys over the years—it was *their* dedication that built this league into what it is today."

"And don't think this is something new." Jiggy's voice filled with emotion. "This has been going on in Rockland since I was their age. Johnny's dad, *Chick* Gallo, was *our* mentor. Back in the thirties and forties, he organized us into Rockland's first competitive baseball program. All through the Depression years, he made us believe that we were just as good as any of those city boys. When he became commissioner of this new league eight years ago, it was his dream that we would bring back the program and someday put Rockland on *top* of the baseball mountain. And it's his legacy that we've passed along to these boys today."

Jiggy was sobbing now as the old commissioner joined him on the stage. Heritage and pride filled the room. There wasn't a dry eye in the house.

"These uniforms our boys are wearing," he continued, "that ball field that they play on, the thousands of volunteer hours that the baseball men of this town have given them: it was all for *one* reason. It was all to give them a first-class opportunity to be their best. And tonight we saw the fruits of all that labor.

"That's all I wanted to say. Good night, thank you and God bless these boys."

It was bedlam as we made our way through the crowd, shaking hands with men, being kissed by women, being hugged by all my relatives, who seemed to be everywhere. I finally reached Molly near the doorway. It was nearly eleven o'clock and her parents were dragging her out to the car to go home. "You were great tonight," she shouted over the noise.

"I struck out," I shouted back. "I could have cost us the game." She just shook her head slowly and took my arm. "No," she whispered in my ear, "you were great."

Have I mentioned I was crazy about that girl?

The crowd noise was all around us and her parents were insisting it was time to leave. "You know, I really…"

I wanted to tell her how happy I was, how great I thought *she* was, but I hesitated for a moment, embarrassed by the friends and relatives and well-wishers that surrounded us.

"I know," she said, breaking the silence. "Me too." And just like that, she was gone.

The Rockland police had waived the ten-o'clock curfew for the night and moved it back to midnight. When I told my parents I wanted to walk home, my mom gave me a big kiss goodbye and my dad told me he was proud of me. *Everything is perfect*, I thought. *Everything is just the way it should be.*

I found Tony and Harry, and we made our way out through the thinning crowd and started the long walk home. "Wow," Tony wondered, taking a big sip of his grape Crush as we made our way down the dark streets of Rockland, "do you believe this?"

"Coach Gallo was wrong about the trophies," Harry smiled. "These are *a lot* nicer than the New Galilee trophies." We all held up our golden prizes. He was right; these trophies were almost a foot tall and had a wooden base with a gold stand, then a long, carved wooden loving cup and a golden batter on top.

At the start of the New Castle Tournament, more than five hundred ballplayers dreamed of winning the trophies we held in our hands right now. They put the New Galilee awards to shame.

"He just said that because he didn't *really* think we could win in New Castle," Tony speculated. "Nobody thought we could win this tournament."

"After the first Beaver Falls game," I chipped in, "is when I thought we could win it all. We just needed to find a way to score."

"But who thought it would be *Harry* that got the big hit?" Tony deadpanned. "You lucky bastard, you really came through."

"That pitch could have been anywhere." Harry stopped for a second and shook his head. "I was swinging no matter where it was. But it just came right down the middle. When I hit it, I started praying it would stay fair and find the ground before anyone could reach it. Then I saw it land inside the foul line, and I just felt like I was flying. I don't even remember touching first. The next thing I knew I was laying there on the ground, hugging second base, and the sound, it was like thunder, and I looked up and everything was glowing."

"All right, hero," Tony smirked. "Don't get *too* carried away. This wasn't the World Series and you're not Mazeroski."

"I saw Alice Landers giving you the goo-goo eyes in there," I taunted him. "I guess you're *her* hero now."

"She's cute," Harry shrugged. "And Pam and Molly looked great too, but it won't be long before we forget these Rockland girls. I mean in two more years I'll be going to high school in Ellwood City, and in four years, I'll be driving. We can go wherever we want. Do you really think we'll still be dating Rockland girls?"

It was the first time I had ever considered that someday I'd be with someone other than Molly. "I guess you're right," I hesitated. "It doesn't make sense that I'd never date anyone else."

"Don't worry about it, cousin." Tony slapped me on the back. "If you think our girlfriends *now* are beautiful, just imagine what our *wives* are going to look like."

I closed my eyes for a second and tried to imagine her face, but came up empty. "I don't know, Tony," I sighed. "I think we've got it pretty good right now."

"Nope," he answered. "It just gets better from here. It just gets better and better every day and then you die and go to Heaven, and that's just the *best* it can get."

"Maybe *this* is Heaven," I offered. "Right now, right here."

"No, you're wrong," Harry stated matter-of-factly. "It gets better, Teddy. It just keeps getting better. We'll be adults someday. That's got to be like, *ten times* better!"

chapter thirty-five

A Very Good Day

I made my way out of the patient lounge and headed down the hallway back toward Harry's room. I was thinking about the best way to explain the post-game celebration to him: how to best describe the emotion of the town, the pride of our parents, and the pride in ourselves.

"Excuse me, Mr..... uh.... Tresh." I was passing the nurses' station and was surprised to see that the pastel nurse was sitting at the desk, writing notes into the patient files. "Excuse me, Mr. Tresh," she repeated. "May I see you?"

I walked toward the sliding windows in the middle of the glass cubicle. Of course the bottom half of the nurses' station was plaster and hardwood, but from about four feet to the ceiling it was glass. Patients accessed staff members through the sliding windows above the counter.

"Sure," I said. "What can I do for you?"

"How much do you know about your friend Harry's condition?" she sighed. "Do you know he has organic brain injuries?"

"I knew he had brain damage from the fever, but I really didn't know what to expect."

"In Harry's case," she confided, "you shouldn't expect too much."

"Actually, I thought he'd be much worse," I contradicted her. "I'm very happy that he seems sharp and with it and even witty sometimes."

"Well, this has been a good day for Mr. Kirkland, a very good day. He used to have them pretty often, but now it's only once or twice a month. It seems like now he just loses himself for weeks at a time and we practically have to lead him around like a child." She leaned over and whispered the rest. "It's dementia, Mr. Tresh, and it's probably going to get worse, maybe much worse. I just thought you should know."

I made my way back to Harry's room and sat back in the fake-leather chair.

Is she right? I wondered. *Does he really walk around like a zombie ninety percent of the time?*

Then how can I reach him? I shook my head in disappointment. *How can I get him to remember some little part of who he was and what he meant to us? What can he latch onto and hold onto when the darkness comes again?*

Now I heard the unmistakable sound of the approaching patients returning from dinner and started to panic. *Don't think about it*, I urged myself. *Just finish the story. Start with the parade and go from there.*

I stood up as Harry and James entered the room together. James was leading Harry by the arm and Harry was staring down at his own feet as he walked to his bed and sat on the edge.

"Well, are you ready to hear about the celebration, buddy?" I said, jumping up from the chair. Harry looked up at me in alarm.

The shocked expression on his face was surprising. Did he think I hadn't waited for him, that I would be gone by now?

"When we got back to town, there were fire engines and police cars waiting for us," I began. But something made me stop.

Harry's eyes looked completely vacant and terrified, like a small child lost in a supermarket. Then his expression slowly shifted from terrified to familiar to friendly. "Hey," he said. "I know you. You're Teddy Tresh. I *know* you!"

I studied his face for a long minute. There was no humor, no sarcasm, and no wit in his comments. He simply was surprised to see me.

I felt a twitch in my stomach and a sudden burning in my forehead. "I'm sorry," I said, backing away from Harry and his roommate. "Can you excuse me for a second?" I stepped inside Harry's small bathroom with the polished-steel mirror and the two-way, push-button door-lock and vomited into the sink.

After a few minutes I composed myself, washed out my mouth with water from the tap, and stepped back into the room.

The pastel nurse was waiting for me inside Harry's room. "Mr. Kirkland, I think your guest should go now." Harry just stood there grinning.

"Wait," I said, holding up the framed news clipping for a moment and then placing it in Harry's hands. "I want to give this to him first."

"No," Harry answered, with a flash of recognition. "Everything in here gets destroyed. You take this back home and give it to your son, so he can know what we did."

"All right, Harry, I'll take the picture frame," I nodded, "if you promise to try your best to remember us." I took it from him and started toward the door, then stopped. "Harry, do you know me?"

"I remember you," he blurted. "You're Teddy Tresh, my friend."

"Will you do me a favor?" I asked, my voice cracking with every word. "Every time you think of me or Tony DeVito or Jiggy or Derrick Dawson, I want you to remember that we were all heroes for a while; we were champions and you were one of us. You're a hero, Harry," I repeated. "Don't forget that."

"I'll remind him," laughed Big James as he began bouncing and shadow-boxing with Harry. "Who's a hero?" he barked at Harry, who looked at him blankly. "Who's the champ?"

"Um... I'm the champ," Harry offered feebly.

"That's right," snarled James, still boxing and weaving, "You the champ... *You* the champ."

Harry finally broke into a smile.

I stepped forward, shook his hand and gave him a brief hug, and then turned and walked out toward the elevator. The pastel nurse followed me all the way to the doors and waited as I got inside. "You shouldn't be upset, Mr. Tresh. Harry had a good day today, a very good day."

I don't remember the elevator ride downstairs or the walk to my car. The first thing I was cognizant of after leaving Harry was watching Mayview Hospital disappear in my rearview mirror. "Breathe in, breathe out," was all I was thinking. "Breathe in, breathe out." Finally I felt some color coming back into my cheeks.

My head was spinning like a giant whirlpool and I could clearly see the hopelessness of Harry's life. It hurt to think, so I tried not to. Instead I tried to distract myself with some other thought; any other thought.

Finally I looked down at the yellow legal pad I had lying next to me in the passenger seat. There was a list of five business prospects I was supposed to visit on this trip to Bridgeville. *Shit*, I thought, *I got nothing done today. My boss is going to kill me.* The familiar fear of being behind schedule snapped me back to the light of day.

I set my mind to the problem at hand. It was nearly six o'clock now and I just wanted to get home, but if I had any chance of catching up on my workload before morning, I needed to stop back at the office and grab some files. My biggest concern was: if my boss was still in his office, he'd question me about every prospect on that list.

I started to cook up some likely scenarios. "This car dealer was out of town. This attorney wanted more information regarding TV advertising. This auto body shop is committed to newspaper advertising." One by one I came up with some lame delaying tactic for each prospect.

I had been working for TCI Cable Company for about eighteen months, ever since I moved my family back to Western Pennsylvania from Boston. My sales had been great for the first year, but there was no use making waves if I didn't need to.

When I reached our headquarters, everything was dark except for the sales manager's office. Just as I feared, my boss, Jim Hartman, was still at work completing his weekly sales report.

"How'd it go with Classic Chevrolet?" he sang out from his desk as I walked by.

"Great," I told him. "They liked your idea of promoting themselves as the country's oldest Chevy dealer. They renewed their contract for another six months."

"Tremendous," he answered, inviting me to take a chair at his desk. "You're really on fire. How did you do on those prospecting calls in Bridgeville?"

I looked down at my notes on the yellow legal pad, all the lies I had written there. I paused for a second and studied my boss' face. He was about the same age as me, but thinner, lankier, more animated. When he walked, he looked like a puppet on a string, all hands and arms and feet swinging in different directions.

I tried to imagine him at ten or twelve years old, standing in the batter's box, trying to hit Dawson or Fontaine. *He'd have no chance*, I thought. *He'd be completely helpless.*

In the back of my head I could hear Uncle Joe's voice: "Do your talking on the field."

I looked down at the yellow pad again and then stuffed it into my briefcase. "I didn't make any prospecting calls today," I said finally. "When I left Classic Chevy, I noticed how close I was to Mayview Hospital. So I decided to drop in and visit an old friend of mine. He had a bout with viral encephalitis when he was twenty-nine. It left him with permanent brain damage. He's been in a mental institution ever since."

"Jesus." Hartman shook his head with concern. "How's he doing now?"

"He looks like he's eighty," I replied. "But I guess he has some good days. I think he enjoyed the visit."

As I drove home that night, I thought about Harry, a man with no past and no identity. I wondered if the story I told him would have any long-term effect; if he could hold onto some little slice of pride, or if he would just continue to spiral toward death, trapped there in his little hell.

What had the nuns called it—*Purgatory?*

"It's just like Hell," they used to teach us, "except you still have hope. You still know that someday your suffering is going to end; that someday you'll be in Heaven with God."

I hope they're right, I thought.

It was one of those church stories that had a *true* ring to it, like God coming to earth as a poor child, being born in a stable and lying in a manger. *If it's not true, it ought to be*, I told myself. *It* ought *to be true.*

chapter thirty-six

What Heaven Holds

I looked out my hotel window into the crowded streets of the city below: at the open space in the skyline that, just fifteen months earlier, had been home to the twin towers of the World Trade Center. Five years had passed since I last saw Harry. The city and the entire country were just beginning the long process of healing.

I was in Manhattan with my wife, Lynn. Her company had sent her to New York on a business trip and instead of flying home on Friday, I told her to get us a room for the weekend and I would fly out there. It was January 2003, just a week before her birthday. So we had planned to celebrate by hitting a nice restaurant in Soho on Friday night and then seeing the Billy Joel musical *Moving Out* on Broadway on Saturday.

I had already taken my shower and was sitting on the edge of the bed staring at the empty void in the sky as Lynn dried her hair in the bathroom. The shrill sound of the hairdryer was suddenly interrupted by the even-shriller sound of my cell phone crackling out the theme song from *Peter Gunn*. "Hello," I answered.

"Where are you?" my mother's voice sputtered from the earpiece.

"I'm in New York," I reminded her. "Remember, I told you we were getting away for the weekend?"

"Oh, that's nice," she sang. "But listen, I have some bad news. Harry Kirkland died. He was only fifty years old."

It hit me like an ocean wave of guilt and regret and sadness. I paused for a moment.

"Teddy!" she shouted after a few seconds. "Teddy—are you still there?"

"I'm here, Mom," I spoke up finally.

"Oh, I thought I lost you," she moaned, "I've been having so much trouble with this phone." My mother had had trouble with every phone she ever owned since they replaced her rotary phone in 1979.

"When did he die, Mom… how?"

"He died in *that* hospital." It sounded like she was describing a soap opera. "He never came home."

"Well, I guess he's home now." I told her.

"The paper says pneumonia." She was reading now. "Visiting hours are from 7 to 9 p.m. tomorrow only."

"Oh, man…" I groaned, "There's no way I can get back. I just got here and it's Lynn's birthday and we have tickets to a Broadway show."

"They won't expect you to go," my mother said comfortingly. "Nobody's even seen Harry in twenty years."

"I saw him," I said. "I saw him five years ago and I don't want his mother to think that I'm just some other Rockland kid who forgot about him."

I wrapped up the conversation with my mother as quickly as I could, which was probably another ten to fifteen minutes. Lynn had come back into the room and was starting to get dressed. She could tell by my half of the phone conversation that something was wrong.

As I hung up my cell phone, she looked at me expectantly. "Harry Kirkland's dead," I sighed. "I never even went back to visit him."

"You're one of the few who ever *did* visit him," she said, sitting down beside me on the bed. Lynn always tried to protect me from criticism, even if *I* was the one doing the criticizing. We had been together for twenty-five years, ever since the day she walked into our high-school journalism class. She was the sweetest thing I'd ever seen. The fact that she stood by me unconditionally was the cherry on the sundae.

"Are you going to the funeral?" she said. She was just letting me know it was okay if I wanted to go.

"No," I whispered. "There's no way I can go home now. I don't really even *want* to go. I just don't want Harry's family to think that no one cared about him."

"Call his mother," Lynn suggested. "Tell her why you can't be there and express your regrets."

Lynn always seemed to know exactly the right thing to do. "I actually *remember* his mother's phone number," I nodded. "It's only one number different from *my* mom's number. We used to be on a party line. We knew more about the Kirklands than we ever cared to know," I smiled as I punched in the digits.

"Hi, Janie," I started when she answered the call. "It's Ted Tresh."

"Oh, Teddy," she sighed, "I guess you heard the news."

"I'm so sorry for your loss," I offered. "I'm in New York City and my mom just called to let me know."

"He's in a better place," she continued. "He was bad at the end, Teddy. He didn't even recognize us."

I hesitated. "I'm sure on some level he knew you were there for him and that he wasn't alone. Listen, Janie, I just got to New York and I'm not going to be able to make it back for the funeral. I'm really sorry.

"I go to so many wakes for people I hardly know," I went on, "But I really care about *this* one. I'm sorry I can't get back for Harry. I wanted you to know my thoughts are with you and your wonderful family."

As I hung up the phone, Lynn sat down on the bed beside me and put her head on my shoulder. "I'm sorry about your friend," she said. "We can fly back tonight if you want to."

I just shook my head. "There's no use. He's not really there," I told her. "He's finally free. His suffering is over."

She didn't say a word. She just held on tighter.

"When he had the attack and lost his memory, I always knew that he lost *his* identity. But I guess I didn't realize that I lost part of my identity too."

I buried my face in her soft brown hair. "All those years… It was Tony and Harry and me. We fed off each other. Our egos and self-esteem were all tied up together. Then he got the fever and part of who we were was lost. I guess I felt guilty that we went on and he was left behind. But maybe tonight he got his identity back, and maybe I got part of mine back too."

"He's in a better place," she said without looking up.

"Oh, I know where Harry is," I chuckled. "He's in the batter's box at Dean Park. There're no balls and two strikes and he just lined a shot into the right-field corner. There's a roar from the crowd as he rounds first and heads to second. He dives into second base headfirst and then gets up and looks toward the dugout. Everything is glowing and the cheering is like thunder.

"Harry's finally home."

chapter thirty-seven

Epilogue: The Street Lamp

There was a time before heartbreak and sickness and death; before failures and losses and broken relationships; before we had to make up excuses for why God allows terrible things to happen, because terrible things *never did* happen, not to us, not yet.

On the best night of their lives, three Little Leaguers in red-trimmed uniforms walk home together down the dark streets of Rockland. They're carrying golden trophies and laughing like drunken soldiers.

"Life just gets better and better," Harry is saying. "We'll be driving soon and we can go wherever we want to go and we can see whoever we want to see."

I shake my head in disagreement. "Things are perfect right now," I argue. "How can they get any better? Did I tell you what the Beaver Falls coach said about us?" I'm beaming now. "He said they couldn't score on Dawson and that *damn* red infield. That's *us*. He was talking about *us*."

We stop under a streetlight at the corner of Fourth Avenue and Main Street and linger for a moment or two; just three Little Leaguers on the best night of their lives, glowing under the streetlamp, a crystal-clear vision suspended in time.

"What do you want to do tomorrow?" Tony asks finally.

"Come over to my house in the morning," I answer. "Maybe we'll pick up a game."

ABOUT THE AUTHOR

ED PRENCE is a successful businessman who graduated with a degree in Journalism from Duquesne University in 1978 while playing four years of college baseball as a Division I shortstop. Ed splits his time between conducting youth baseball clinics and traveling the world, and still roots for his favorite team, the hapless Pittsburgh Pirates.

Made in the USA
Charleston, SC
13 April 2013